Something was going on. Something that was putting a six-year-old kid in danger. Dallas wanted to find out what, and he wanted to know exactly how Carly had gotten involved in it.

"We need to speak with the police."

"I can't do that."

"Why not?"

"If they find out I've gone to the police, they'll take my son. I'll never see him again."

"Is that what they told you?"

"Yes."

Somewhere in the deepest part of the shadows, a twig snapped. He grabbed Carly's hand and dragged her into thick undergrowth.

Someone was out there with them.

A phone buzzed, the sound a discordant note in the eerie silence. He gestured for Carly to turn the thing off but she was staring at the screen.

"We need to go," she said, trying to dart past him.

There was something about the tension in her face that made him glance at the text she'd opened, the photo it contained. A kid staring out from behind a window, his dark curly hair a lot like Carly's.

"They're going to take Zane. I'll never see him again," Carly said, her voice trembling. "They're outside of my house, watching him."

Aside from her faith and her family, there's not much **Shirlee McCoy** enjoys more than a good book! When she's not teaching or chauffeuring her five kids, she can usually be found plotting her next Love Inspired Suspense story or wandering around the beautiful Inland Northwest in search of inspiration. Shirlee loves to hear from readers. If you have time, drop her a line at shirlee@shirleemccoy.com.

Books by Shirlee McCoy

Love Inspired Suspense

Mission: Rescue

Protective Instincts
Her Christmas Guardian
Exit Strategy
Deadly Christmas Secrets
Mystery Child
The Christmas Target
Mistaken Identity
Christmas on the Run

Classified K-9 Unit

Bodyguard

Rookie K-9 Unit

Secrets and Lies

Capitol K-9 Unit

Protection Detail
Capitol K-9 Unit Christmas
"Protecting Virginia"

Visit the Author Profile page
at Harlequin.com for more titles.

CHRISTMAS ON THE RUN

SHIRLEE MCCOY

HARLEQUIN® LOVE INSPIRED® SUSPENSE

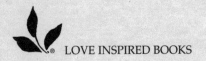 LOVE INSPIRED BOOKS

Recycling programs
for this product may
not exist in your area.

ISBN-13: 978-0-373-45740-3

Christmas on the Run

www.Harlequin.com

Printed in U.S.A.

Lord, your love is as high as the heavens.
Your faithful love reaches up to the skies. Your holiness
is as great as the height of the highest mountains.
You are honest as the oceans are deep. Lord, you
keep people and animals safe. How priceless your faithful
love is! People find safety in the shadow of your wings.
—*Psalms* 36:5-7

To you. I hope, as you read this dedication, you smile.

ONE

Feet pounding, lungs heaving, sweat dripping down her temples, Carly Rose Kelley raced along the paved path that led deep into Rock Creek Park. Up ahead, an ancient metal bridge traversed the Little Patuxent River, its solid beams rusted red from years exposed to the elements, its joists gleaming dully in the predawn light. The bridge was a remnant of a railroad that had been defunct for decades—tough, old, used up, but somehow still fighting to survive.

Exactly like Carly.

Except she wasn't old. She'd be thirty-three in five days. And it wasn't her life she was fighting for. It was Zane's.

Zane—gift from God. An unexpected one. She and Josh hadn't wanted kids. They'd both had too much baggage, they'd traveled more than they were home and they'd had goals that hadn't included slowing down to care for a child.

But Zane had come along anyway.

Carly would do anything for him, but she wouldn't be blackmailed, she wouldn't be bullied and she wouldn't be forced to go against her moral code. She could keep her son safe and still do the right thing. She *would* keep him safe.

God, please help me keep him safe.

She reached the bridge, the old metal shaking under her feet as she pounded across it. She knew they'd be behind her, that in a minute or two or three, she'd hear metal clanging as they crossed the tributary.

She didn't look back.

There'd be nothing to see, just a couple of shadowy figures trailing behind her, making sure she knew she was being watched. All day, every day. All night. It seemed that everywhere she went, they were there. Zane was their bargaining chip: *Do what we tell you, or he'll disappear one day and you'll never see him again. Maybe not tomorrow or next week or even next year, but one day, he'll leave the house and he won't come home.*

She shuddered, the sick dread she'd been feeling for two months welling up.

Call the police and he dies. Tell anyone, and you'll never see him again.

Do what we say, and everything will be fine.

She didn't believe the last part, but she'd been co-operating because of the photos of Zane at day camp, at school, at music lessons. They'd been slipped under her door at work, emailed to her, dropped in the mail slot at the beautiful brownstone she'd bought in DC. She'd installed a security camera, but all she'd caught was the image of a person with a hat pulled low over his eyes, walking up her porch steps like he belonged there.

Yeah. She'd been *cooperating*, biding her time, trying to come up with a plan that would keep her son safe. After the first phone call, she'd lain in bed every night for nearly three weeks, praying and begging and trying not to cry, because she'd escaped poverty, crime, a heroin-addicted mother and a career-criminal father only to come to another place of danger and insecurity. She'd known that crying wouldn't help, so she hadn't shed a tear. She'd focused on solving the problem and escaping the situation. She'd managed it as a teenager. She could manage it now. That was what she'd told herself during the long dark hours before dawn. The way she'd seen things, she'd had only two options to keep her son safe—go to the police and hope for the best, or go into hiding, giving up everything she'd worked so hard for. She'd been leaning toward the latter option, because she'd rather give up everything than risk Zane's life.

Then she'd remembered the box that she'd carried from one rental house to the next for the past five years. She hadn't had any use for the stuff inside, but she'd thought that Zane might want it one day. Her husband Josh's birth certificate. His adoption decree. An antique pendant he'd grabbed from his mother's jewelry box before he'd left home for good—or, rather, been kicked out because he'd stolen five thousand dollars from his parents to buy drugs and alcohol. He hadn't been proud of it, but he'd figured it was his parents' fault. They could have been more patient, more understanding, more aware of how it felt to be an unwanted tween adopted by a couple who'd never had kids.

That was what Josh had said.

Typical of him—he hadn't taken responsibility for anything.

By the time he and Carly had met, he'd changed his surname back to what it had been before he was adopted, and he'd put that part of his life behind him.

He'd wanted nothing to do with his parents, but he'd idolized his older half brother, Dallas. According to Josh, Dallas had made every effort to fit in with his adoptive family. He'd done well in school, gone to college and joined the military. He'd also turned his back on his own blood. The brothers hadn't had any contact with each other for years, but Josh had followed Dallas through friends. A year before Josh died, Dallas had left the navy and joined an elite private hostage-rescue team called HEART. An old high school friend had told Josh all about it, and Josh had told Carly. He'd also bragged to anyone willing to listen that Dallas was a hero who traveled all over the world to find the missing and to bring victimized people home to their families.

Yeah, Josh really had loved his brother.

Too bad he hadn't loved Carly. He'd cheated on her, lied to her, taken money from their accounts and used it to buy expensive gifts for other women. Those were things she'd found out after he'd died, and they were things she'd never tell Zane. As far as she was concerned, Josh had been as much of a loser as her parents had been. Just another disappointment in a long list of them, but…

He'd left that box with everything she'd need to get in touch with someone who might be able to help her.

Dallas Morgan.

Decorated war veteran.

Hostage-rescue negotiator. Sharpshooter. Sniper.

If she could contact him without setting off an alarm with the people who were manipulating her, she just might be able to stop them.

Please, God, please, she prayed silently as she raced along the path, the antique pendant, Josh's birth certificate and a handwritten note sealed in a plastic bag and zipped into the small pocket of her running pants. The path veered to the right, and she followed it, catching glimpses of Christmas lights through the trees. This time of year, everything seemed to glow. Houses, stores and streetlights were all decorated for the season.

The beauty of those things always made Carly long for the kind of family she could go home to. The kind of family that exchanged gifts and baked cookies, that sang Christmas carols and attended Christmas Eve service together. This year, more than ever, she wanted that. Not the family she'd grown up with. A family that would stand beside her. One that would be just as determined and desperate to keep Zane safe as she was.

Up ahead, the path was dark, curving through thick tree growth. Dallas's place was five miles away. If she cut through the woods, she'd get there more quickly and avoid some of the dark stretches, but that would make the people following her suspicious.

She was a creature of habit. She couldn't deny it. She'd grown up in chaos; now she liked order, predictability and routine. She left for work at the same time every day. She picked Zane up at school at the same time every afternoon. She went to church every Sunday, grocery shopping every Monday, to the library every Tuesday evening, out with friends exactly once every other week. They knew it.

They knew a lot.

But they didn't know her. If they did, they would have found someone else to do the job, because there was no way she planned to follow through. She had too much integrity, and she was too devoted to the preservation of antique jewelry. Twenty gemstones in four months. That was what they wanted. Polished and cut with antique methods that very few people in the country were familiar with.

Carly was very familiar with them. Some people called her an expert. She called herself a lifelong student. She'd apprenticed under a man who'd made studying and perfecting those methods his life's work. Now it was hers. Aside from working as a museum conservator, she freelanced as an antique-jewelry restoration specialist. She could fix Great-Grandma's Victorian earrings, Aunt Marie's broken mourning ring. She could cut and polish new stones and make them match old ones almost exactly.

She did it to pay the bills and because she hated to see a piece tossed into a drawer or thrown into a scrap pile. With every job she did, she provided documentation that included the date of restoration, the modern gemstones that she'd cut and placed into the piece, and the methods that she'd used. Over the years, she'd worked with high-end jewelry shops and for some very wealthy people. She'd also worked for museums and private collectors. She had a reputation, and that reputation must have put her in the sights of the people who were manipulating her.

But she wasn't a forger. She would not pass her work off as someone else's.

She also wouldn't replace the very expensive and intrinsically valuable gemstones in the Smithsonian collection she was restoring and preserving with her handiwork.

That was what they wanted.

They hadn't said it, but the stones they'd provided her with, the instructions they'd given her for cutting those stones, made it clear that she was re-creating many of the gemstones from Ida May Babcock's gift to the Smithsonian. The oil magnate heiress had died six years ago. She'd had no children, no husband, no connections except for a pet cockapoo that had died three years after her. She *had* had a will and a handful of distant relatives who'd all wanted a piece of her estate. It had taken six years and hundreds of thousands of dollars for her executor to make certain that the will was honored——her wealth and real estate to charities, her art, jewelry and vast collections of antiques to the Smithsonian. Carly had been chosen to itemize the jewelry collection, put together a conservation plan and restore any pieces that needed it.

She'd been thrilled to take the job. Zane was getting older, and her years of traveling the country working contracted jobs had to end. Zane needed stability. He needed neighbors and teachers who knew him from one year to the next. He needed a group of friends that he'd grow up with. He needed everything she'd never had.

But, more than anything, he needed to be safe.

She shuddered, picking up speed as she reached the darkest section of the park. Trees pressed in on either side, the soft rustle of leaves in the winter breeze the only sound.

She ran to the edge of the paved path and turned left onto packed earth. She could hear her feet pounding against the ground, her breath panting out in the same even rhythm. She couldn't hear her pursuers. That was good. It meant they were keeping their distance. Just like always. She'd use that to her advantage. She didn't need to focus on the pace of the run or on the rhythm of her steps. She'd been this way dozens of times before.

She knew the path and the park. She didn't know who was following her. That was a question she asked herself every day. Who? Why?

Someone at the museum?

Someone who knew the value of the jewelry she was working with?

Maybe. She didn't know, and she hadn't dared try to figure it out. She'd felt hunted for weeks, stalked by a nameless, faceless entity. And she wanted it over. Now. Not tomorrow or next week or next month. If Josh's brother wouldn't help, she'd pack her bags and leave in the dead of night. She'd go somewhere she'd never been before, and she'd start a new life doing something that had nothing to do with old jewelry.

Of course, that would mean leaving her life behind.

Leaving Jazz behind.

Jazz. Her best friend from college. The person who'd shown up on her doorstep the day after Josh died and who'd arrived again two weeks before Zane's birth and announced that she planned to stay until after the baby was born. It had ended up being much longer than that. Jazz had been working on establishing herself as a children's book author. She'd needed an affordable home, and Carly had needed someone she trusted to watch Zane while she worked. It had been a perfect arrangement. They were as close as sisters. Jazz was the only aunt Zane had ever known and would ever have. The thought of disappearing and never contacting her again was sickening.

But Jazz was getting married on New Year's Eve. She'd have a great life. Even if Carly and Zane disappeared from it forever.

At least, that was what Carly had been telling herself. It was what she wanted to believe. She couldn't stomach the thought of Jazz mourning them any more than she could stomach the thought of living life without her best friend.

Carly shoved the thoughts way, forcing herself to sink into the rhythm of the run. Frigid November air seeped through the layers of her running gear, freezing sweat onto her skin and making her shiver. Behind her, a twig snapped, and she almost looked back.

Almost.

She didn't want them to see her fear, though. She wouldn't give them the satisfaction.

Her lungs burned, her legs trembled as she sprinted through the park. She'd planned everything, timed it all perfectly. She just had to stick to the plan and keep the goal in mind. She had to focus her energy on getting to Dallas's house and delivering the message she'd brought for him.

Up ahead, bright lights twinkled through the trees, beckoning her toward the well-established neighborhood Dallas lived in. His house was a 1930s brick bungalow on a double lot just yards from the park. He had a mail slot in the front door, large shrubs blocking the view of the side yards. If she ran fast enough and timed it right, she could be up on his porch, sliding the plastic bag into his house, before the people behind her made it off the path.

If…

That was what scared her. She'd been running for years. She knew how to pace herself, and she knew how to go all out for the finish line. But something could go wrong. Life had taught her that early, and it had taught her well.

She sprinted off the trail and around a small pond, the sun lingering below the horizon, the water glass-like in its stillness. She reached the paved path, ran between old houses that had probably been built long before the park existed, turned onto the road that cut through Dallas's neighborhood. She glanced back as she reached the edge of Dallas's yard. The road was empty. Just as she'd known it would be.

Go, go, go!

Her brain shouted the command to her tired legs. She'd been running at her top speed for too long, trying to keep far enough ahead to finish what she'd begun. Now she was tired, but she couldn't stop. She couldn't quit. She unzipped her pocket as she ran, yanking the bag out with trembling hands. If she were cutting a gemstone, she'd have taken a deep breath, tried to still the shaking before she continued, but she didn't have time to calm her nerves.

Dallas's porch light was off. Just like always. One light shone through a window in the upper level. Also just like always. No Christmas lights or decorations. She'd noticed that. Even though all his neighbors had them. Everything was just the way it had been every morning for as long as she'd been running past his place. But something felt off today, the air edged with electricity. She reached the porch stairs, the bag in her hand, her heart beating frantically.

Her watch beeped a warning. One minute gone. She'd practiced this. She knew exactly how long she had before her pursuers arrived, but she'd set her watch anyway. Always thinking ahead. Always planning. Always trying to control things. Josh had told her that hundreds of times. It hadn't been a compliment. Those things had caused conflict in her marriage, but they'd also gotten her through really difficult situations.

Hurry, hurry, hurry!

She darted to the door, shoved the bag through the mail slot and ran back the way she'd come, lungs heaving, sweat cold on her forehead and cheeks. She glanced back at the path. Still nothing. She was almost in the clear. She just had to keep moving.

Across the road, a dark shadow moved out from behind an old tree. Her heart thumped, one hard terrible jolt of acknowledgment. They'd been a step ahead of her after all, and now they knew that she'd tried to pass information to someone.

"What were you doing?" the man said.

Fear shivered through her, made her legs tremble so much she had to stop. Right at the edge of the yard. Nothing separating her from him but a few feet of paved road.

"Back off, buddy." She bit the words out, making sure they dripped with confidence.

"What were you doing?" he asked again, his tone conversational rather than accusatory.

"Running." Her watch beeped again, and she jumped.

Two minutes gone.

Not that it mattered. She'd been caught, and now she had to escape.

She dodged to the left, but he must have anticipated the move, because he was there, blocking her path. Taller by nearly a foot. Muscular. Quick.

She'd grown up fighting. She could still fight when she needed to.

She swung hard with a right hook.

He grabbed her wrist, pulling her arm down with so little effort she knew she'd never escape him.

Not before his buddies made it to her place, found a way in and took her son.

She swung again. This time with her left fist, wildly. She had no plan but to free herself. She connected with his shoulder and heard him mutter something before he pulled her right arm up behind her back. Almost to the point of pain—but not quite.

She stepped toward him, using her body as a weapon, her shoulder aimed for his solar plexus as her watch beeped again.

Dallas Morgan didn't know who the woman was. He didn't know what she wanted. He did know that she'd been running past his house every morning for three weeks. He'd seen her on his security monitor, racing along so close to his front yard that the camera, which had been set up to turn on when there was movement at the edge of the grass, caught her grainy image. Twice she'd jogged to his porch and back, always looking at her watch while she did it. The watch that was beeping.

A warning?

He glanced at the front of his house, expecting an explosion, a fire, something that would make any one of his enemies very happy. And he did have enemies, most of them in foreign countries or in prison. But that didn't mean they couldn't get to him—maybe the scrawny runner was working for one of them.

"Cool it!" he commanded as she tried to hook a leg around his, pull him off balance and free herself.

"Let me go," she growled, wrestling against his hold. His instinct was to do what she'd asked. She was shorter, lighter and weaker than he was, and from the age of twelve on, he'd been taught good manners, good morals and fair rules of combat.

Those things flew out the window when it came to protecting family or staying alive. He tightened his grip. Not enough to be painful, but enough to make her think long and hard about continuing the fight.

"Tell me why you've been running by my place every morning for three weeks, and I will," he said, and she stiffened.

"Dallas?"

"You sound surprised."

"I...am."

"Because you didn't expect to be caught?"

"Because things don't usually turn out that great for me."

"Me being out here is great?" He released his hold and took a step back, trying to see her face in the pre-dawn light. Gaunt. Deep hollows beneath high cheekbones. Dark shadows beneath light-colored eyes. That was about all he could see.

"It's better than the alternative."

"Which is?"

"I put something through the mail slot. That will explain."

She started jogging, heading away from the house. He could have let her go, but there was something about her that worried him, a kind of desperate energy he often saw in clients who were looking for help.

He snagged the back of her running vest, pulling her to a stop. "Save me a trip to the house. Tell me now."

"I'm Carly Rose," she said, as if the name should mean something to him.

"If this is a test, I'm going to fail it, because I've never heard the name before." He cut to the chase. She obviously knew him. She'd obviously been casing his house. He wanted to know why. He wanted to know who had sent her. He wanted to move on with his day, because he had a boatload of physical therapy to get through before he returned to HEART. Five weeks recovering from a torn meniscus, and he was almost cleared to return to work.

He was counting the days, because the house was too quiet, the days too long, the nights even longer with nothing to occupy him.

"Kelley," she added, then he knew, and a half dozen memories of his brother filled his mind.

"Josh's widow," she continued, as if he might be too dense to put it all together.

"I get it." He released her vest, stepped back. She wasn't anything like what he'd have expected. Josh had always gone for blonde, voluptuous. Fake. "What do you want?"

"To leave." She glanced toward the dead-end street. He'd chosen the house because of the privacy and the park that butted up against the yard. Plenty of room to run, hike and bike.

"You looked me up for a reason."

"I…need your help, but I can't explain. There isn't time." Her watch beeped again, and she took off, sprinting into the street and heading toward the end of the road.

He should let her go. Josh had only ever been trouble. Even before they'd entered foster care, before they'd been adopted, before he'd stolen from the only two people who had ever loved them, Josh had been all about getting what he could however he could from whom-ever he could. Dallas had some regrets about their rela-tionship, but not enough to make him want to connect with his widow.

So, yeah, he should let Carly Rose Kelley go, but he was at loose ends, and Christmas was coming. His parents did their best to get his mind off the season. For the past six years, they'd invited friends and fam-ily over to their place for a loud and loving Christmas exchange. Dallas always attended, and then he'd return home to his silent, empty house that should have been filled with the excited squeals of the twins, his wife, maybe another child or two.

Lila had wanted a big family.

He liked to pretend he'd have agreed to that. He wasn't sure, though. He'd never thought he'd be that great of a husband or father. He hadn't planned to be, either, but then he'd met her, and he'd fallen hard and fast. They'd married four months after they'd met, and she'd been pregnant three months later.

If they'd lived, the twins would be turning seven on Christmas Eve.

He shoved the thought and the memories away. He needed distractions this time of year. Carly was the perfect one.

He could still see her, slowing as she reached the end of the street, apparently less frantic now that she'd put some distance between them. There was another entrance to the park in that direction. Maybe she was heading there.

Whatever the case, he planned to follow. At his own pace, because even if he lost sight of her, he could find her again.

That was what he'd spent the past several years doing—finding people, helping them, bringing them home. Something moved in his periphery, and he swung around, saw a guy walking toward him, coming from the same direction Carly had, sauntering like he had nothing but time on his hands. Except he looked sweaty, his hair plastered to his head.

"Morning," he said as he passed, without looking in Dallas's direction. He also stayed near the center of the street, far enough from the houses to keep motion-detecting security lights from being triggered. And he seemed to be following the same path as Carly. Minus the trip to Dallas's porch.

"Cold morning for a walk," Dallas said, and the man stiffened.

"Yeah. It is." He put on a little speed, increasing his pace just enough for it to be noticeable.

"You going anywhere interesting?"

"What's it to you?"

"Just thinking that if you're following the lady, you might want to stop."

"Mind your own business, buddy," the guy growled.

"It's my business when a woman is running alone and she's being followed," he responded.

"You want trouble?" The guy turned, his eyes blazing. The sun had finally drifted above the horizon, the gold-gray light glancing off mud-brown hair and dull blue eyes.

"I'm not going to walk away from it if it comes calling," Dallas replied. Poking the pig. That was what his father called it. It was something Dallas always seemed compelled to do. Something that had gotten him into trouble more times than he could count.

This time was no different.

The guy moved fast, reaching under the hem of his jacket, the motion smooth and practiced. Dallas had seconds to react, to throw himself sideways, pull his Glock. And then the world was exploding into chaos—a woman screaming, a hundred memories filling his mind as he found his mark and fired his first shot.

TWO

She screamed.

She couldn't stop herself.

And then she ran faster, racing away from the man with the gun, the one who'd been following her.

Racing away from Dallas. He was in danger because of her. She could try to deny it. She could tell herself all kinds of pretty lies, but if he'd been shot, it was because she'd dragged him into trouble. She glanced over her shoulder, stumbling as she reached the transition between pavement and park path.

Nothing in the street. No sign of Dallas. No guy with a gun. Lights had come on in a few houses, and she could hear sirens in the distance. Someone had called the police. She could stay and tell them what she'd seen. She could talk to them about the gemstones she was supposed to be cutting, the threats against Zane. She could put her faith and trust in fallible human beings and an overburdened criminal justice system.

Or she could keep going and leave Dallas to face the consequence of her decisions. She could let him talk to the police, explain what he'd seen, what she'd said.

And while he was doing that, she could be packing and leaving town.

But if he'd been shot…

She stopped, eyeing the empty street, the lit houses, the rising sun glinting off winter-bare trees. Nothing moved, and she took a step back the way she'd come, because she couldn't just abandon Dallas. No matter how much she might want to.

She stopped in front of his house, scanning the yard, looking for signs that he'd been injured. She found what might have been a splotch of blood on the pavement, another drop of it a few inches away. But there was no one lying bleeding on the ground. There was nothing but the gold-gray light of dawn, the chilly winter breeze and the sound of screaming sirens.

She found more blood on the grass, and she followed the trail of it around Dallas's house and across the field that separated his property from the park. The police would arrive soon, and she shouldn't be there when they did. She'd blown it. She'd made that first cut in the stone and she'd gone too deep, pushed too hard. There was nothing to do when that happened but scrap the old plan and come up with a new one.

But she couldn't leave until she knew Dallas was okay. This was her fault, her trouble coming to call on him.

She should have thought about that before she'd taken the chance, but she'd been desperate to keep Zane safe, and Dallas had seemed like the kind of guy who could hold his own in a battle. On paper, he'd even looked like a hero. Not that she believed in those. The fantasy of a white knight riding to her rescue had died about three months after she'd married Josh, right around the time she'd seen a florist receipt on the floor of their closet. *For his mother.*

She'd believed the lie because she'd wanted to, but she'd never again believed he was everything he'd pretended to be.

But those were thoughts for another time.

Right now, she needed to find Dallas and make sure he was okay. Once she did that, she'd do what she should have a month ago. Plan B: leave town, her life, her career. Leave Jazz.

Zane would be devastated. Especially with Christmas coming. It was his favorite holiday. He loved all the traditions. More than anything, he loved having his little family together. Not this year, though. This year Jazz was going to be with her fiancé's family, starting new traditions. Zane had cried when he'd found out. He'd cry more when he realized that he was never going to see his aunt Jazzy again.

But he'd be alive. He'd be safe.

That was what mattered.

She pushed through a thicket and found herself on the trail she'd run in on. No blood there, and the earth was too packed for footprints to be visible. She crouched, searching the ground for any sign that Dallas had been there. The sirens stopped abruptly, and she knew the police had arrived. They were probably questioning whoever had called in the report of gunfire. It wouldn't be long before they found the blood. They might call in a K-9 unit and extra manpower, and she'd be out in the woods, ready to be found and questioned.

Don't go to the police. Don't tell anyone.

She hadn't gone to the police, but she had tried to

tell someone, and now the police were closing in. The people who'd been following her had to know it.

Fear zipped through her, the metallic taste of it filling her mouth. While she was tromping around in the woods looking for Dallas, the people who'd been threatening her could be knocking on the door at her place, making up some excuse for entering the premises.

"Dallas?" she called quietly, the word barely carrying on the morning air.

There was no response. She hadn't really expected there to be.

The blood, the silence. He was injured. Or worse.

And it was her fault.

"Dalla—"

A hand slapped over her mouth, and she was pulled back against a rock-solid chest, her arms pinned to her sides by someone much larger and stronger than she was. She'd learned to fight the same way she'd learned to run, because she'd had no choice. It was that or be used and abused and tossed onto the side of the road like garbage.

She went lax, her weight dropping against her attacker's arm.

When that didn't loosen his grip, she went for his instep, shifting her weight and stomping down hard.

"Stop," he hissed in her ear. "It's Dallas, and there's some guy with a gun wandering around out here. You want him to hear us?"

She shook her head, and his hand slipped from her mouth.

"Are you hurt?" she whispered, trying to turn, but his arm was still locked around her, and she couldn't move.

"Quiet," he said, his lips nearly touching her ear, his

warm breath tickling the hair near her temple. She could feel the heat of his body through her vest and T-shirt, the strength of his muscles against her arms and abdomen. It had been a long time since she'd been physically close to a man, and if his grip hadn't been viselike, she'd have jerked away immediately.

"He's gone," Dallas finally said, releasing his hold and stepping away from her.

"Who?" she asked, turning so they were facing each other. He was taller than she'd thought. Much taller than Josh had been. Probably six-two or -three.

"You tell me," he responded, his eyes an odd green-blue that seemed to glow in the dim morning light.

"How would I know?" she asked.

"You said you needed my help, Carly. Two minutes later some guy I've never seen before took a potshot at me. You knowing something about him seems like a logical conclusion."

She couldn't deny it, and she couldn't waste time discussing it. "I need to go."

"So you said, but here you are, still hanging around in the park."

"I was looking for you. I thought you were hurt, and I was worried that…"

"What?"

"That you'd been shot and it was my fault," she admitted.

"Why would it be your fault?" he asked, circling the conversation back around to get the information he wanted. But she didn't know who the guy with the gun was. If she did, she'd have gone to the police long ago.

"It's a long story. I don't have time to tell it. I left you a note. Read it. Decide what you want to do about it, if you want to do anything, but right now I have to get to my son."

"*Your* son?" he asked, and she heard the hidden question, the words he didn't say.

"Mine and Josh's."

His face went blank, every bit of anger and annoyance seeping from his eyes.

He hadn't known.

Of course he hadn't. Just like with everything else, Josh had lied about telling his brother about the baby.

"He said he told you," she said into the awkward silence, and his jaw tightened.

"Josh said a lot of things that weren't true."

"I know."

"So maybe you could have made sure his family knew about the baby instead of believing him." He started walking away, and she should have done the same, but she felt the desperate need to make him understand, because she needed his help. She needed it more than she'd ever needed just about anything else.

"I didn't have contact information for your parents, and I only found contact information for you after Josh died."

He just kept walking.

"I sent you a note when he passed away. You sent a signed card with no indication that you wanted anything to do with me."

He stopped short. "I know what I sent. I figured you were like every other woman he'd ever dated."

"What's that supposed to mean?"

"Nothing anymore. He's gone. You're here, and you're telling me I have a nephew. You're also telling me you need help, but you're not saying anything about what kind of help."

"I...can't. Not here."

"Then I can't help you."

He was walking again, and she was just standing there watching him go, because she couldn't tell him what was going on, how much was at stake, how scared she was. The words were stuck in her throat, the threats she'd been hearing for two months echoing through her mind.

"Dallas," she said, her voice raspy and harsh.

"What?"

She might have answered—she might have told him everything—but her phone buzzed, and she glanced at the caller ID, sure it was Jazz asking why she was out running in twenty-degree weather.

Only it wasn't Jazz.

It was him.

Unknown caller. Texting words that made her breath catch, her heart stop.

I hope you kissed your son goodbye last night.

Her breath caught, the veiled threat filling her with terror. She hadn't shared anything with Jazz, hadn't even hinted at the trouble she was in. Jazz wouldn't be on guard, because she wouldn't be expecting trouble. Fingers shaking, she texted her friend, telling her to keep Zane inside until she got home. She'd explain when she got there.

She didn't wait for a response. She didn't bother explaining to Dallas. She needed to get home to her son before it was too late.

* * *

Dallas needed to talk to the police. He'd discharged his weapon, and he'd obviously hit the perp. He'd seen the blood, but the guy had moved fast, running between houses and preventing Dallas from getting another clear shot. He hadn't wanted to risk a bullet going through an exterior wall and injuring someone. He'd sprinted after the guy instead, his bum knee keeping him from going full-out. He'd turned around at the path, worried about Carly, concerned that she might be heading straight toward the perp. And, of course, she had been.

And now she was on the move again, sprinting along the path, her long-legged stride even and practiced. She was a runner for sure, an athlete. Young. Pretty.

A mother. And Dallas was an uncle.

If what she'd said was true. He didn't know her, hadn't been invited to the wedding, hadn't received anything but a cursory email from Josh that said he'd been married. By the time he'd received Carly's note about Josh's death, it had been too late to attend the funeral. Even if it hadn't been, Dallas had been in no shape to travel. He'd been in the hospital recovering from the car accident that had taken the lives of Lila and the twins. He'd spent three weeks there, the burns on his arms and chest healing a lot more quickly than his heartache ever would.

Josh's death had been a tiny pinprick of pain compared to the agony of losing his wife and unborn children.

He shook the thought away, concentrating on the run and on keeping his gait even. Carly was sprinting west along a dirt trail that wound its way to one of several parking lots, running like her life depended on it. If he hadn't been so much taller than her, he and his bum knee might have had trouble catching up. As it was, he caught up to her on the first hill, his knee twinging with pain as he matched her pace. His doctor wouldn't be happy. His physical therapist would read him the riot act, but he wasn't going to let Carly head off into the sunrise while an armed man wandered the park.

He grabbed her arm, pulling her to a stop.

"Let go," she muttered, tugging away.

"Running isn't going to solve your problems," he said, and she swung around, her face white, eyes blazing. He'd been afraid she'd be crying, but she looked angry, her words hard and staccato.

"Neither is staying. Go back home, Dallas. I never should have tried to contact you."

"You didn't try. You did contact me."

"It was a mistake."

"Mistakes can't be unmade," he replied, and the muscles in her jaw tightened, her lips pressing together. "You came to me, Carly," he continued. "So did some guy with a gun. I want to know who he is and what he wants."

"I told you—"

"Nothing. Except that you left me a note. And that I have a nephew. Do you think I'm going to forget about him now that I know?"

"I think that you're not going to believe he's your nephew until I offer proof," she countered, swinging around to run again.

"Josh didn't want kids," he responded, because it was true, and because he wanted to push a little harder, force her to give him the information he needed.

Behind them, the woods were filling with voices as the police hunted for the person who'd left the blood trail. He'd need to check in with them. If he didn't, his boss, Chance Miller, would want to know why he hadn't. As a member of the hostage-rescue team, Dallas had an obligation to follow protocol. Even when he wasn't on duty.

"Sometimes we don't get what we want," Carly panted. "Sometimes we get what we don't want. Zane is Josh's son. He's your nephew. And he needs me. I have to go home."

"You left him alone?"

"Of course not! He's only six!"

"There are plenty of people who leave kids younger than that at home alone."

"I'm not one of them. He's with my friend, and… I'm worried." They'd reached the end of the dirt path and pounded onto a paved one, their steps in sync, their breathing almost synchronized, her gasping breaths matching his steadier ones almost perfectly.

She was obviously a long-distance runner, but he doubted she was a sprinter. She was slowing, the speed zapping her energy. He slowed with her, his body humming with adrenaline as he scanned the woods to either side, looking for a glint of metal, a subtle movement. The perp would be a fool to stick around when the police were so close, but people were often willing to be fools if the cause was important enough, what they stood to gain big enough.

"You're worried about the guy with the gun," he said.

She nodded but didn't speak, every bit of her energy pouring into muscles that he could see trembling.

She was done, but she'd keep going. Whatever was driving her—her son, her fear, her need to escape Dallas—forced her to continue. He grabbed her arm again. Gently, because his adoptive father, Timothy Morgan, had taught him how real men were supposed to treat women. It had taken him a couple of years to learn the lesson, to understand that true strength lay in gentleness, calmness, kindness. Once he'd learned it, he hadn't forgotten. Sometimes, though…sometimes he reverted to the troubled inner-city kid who'd walked into the Morgans' suburban home carrying nothing but a plastic bag filled with old clothes.

She jerked away, stumbling as she accidentally stepped off the pavement and onto icy grass.

"Stop," he said as gently as he'd grabbed her arm. His work gave him plenty of practice calming frantic people. He'd dealt with parents who'd lost kids, spouses who'd lost partners, people desperate to find friends, neighbors, lovers. He knew how to keep his voice steady and his approach soft.

"I can't," she said, her voice breaking. There were no tears in her eyes or on her cheeks, but she was on the verge of losing it.

"Eventually, you'll have to."

"Not until I'm home."

"What's your address?" he asked, studying her face, trying to find some hint of who she was, what she really wanted. All he saw was a woman who shouldn't have been his brother's widow. She was too young, too tired, too skinny. Too desperate. Josh's widow should have been full figured, smiling, made-up and fake. She wouldn't have had a care in the world, and she sure as anything wouldn't have had a son.

"I told you, I made a mistake contacting you," she panted.

"I'm sure you remember my response."

"I don't have time to play games, Dallas."

"Neither do I. You said you needed my help. I plan to give it."

She shrugged, rattling off an address in DC. He knew the neighborhood. It was part of a revitalization project designed to beautify the city. Not far from HEART, and filled with young professionals who loved the hustle and bustle of city life, young families who enjoyed the community vibe, older men and women who were on their own and loving it. It was the kind of neighborhood he and Lila had planned to live in until they'd found out she was pregnant. Then they'd chosen a cute house in the suburbs halfway between his parents and hers. They'd decorated the nursery yellow because Lila hadn't wanted to know the gender of the babies. He tried not to think about that or about the way she'd looked when she'd picked him up from the airport that last night— her belly softly rounded and pressing against the pink sweater she wore. She'd been six months pregnant and glowing with it. He'd told her that she'd never looked more beautiful.

He released Carly's arm, pulled out his cell phone and sent a text to his boss, shoving aside all the old memories and focusing on the present. That was how he'd survived the first year, and it was how he continued to survive.

The Lord giveth and the Lord taketh away.

Only Dallas hadn't been ready to let Him take anything, and he'd spent most of the past few years trying to get over the anger and bitterness the loss had caused.

Chance replied to his text, promising to send someone over to Carly's place to keep an eye on things. He also asked for an explanation.

Later was all Dallas offered. Something was going on. Something that was putting a six-year-old kid in danger. He wanted to find out what, and he wanted to know exactly how Carly had gotten involved in it. Maybe she was an innocent bystander who'd been pulled into something, or maybe she was responsible for the trouble she'd found herself in.

Either way, he planned to keep the kid safe.

If there was a kid.

He slid the phone back in his pocket, made certain his Glock was hidden beneath his jacket and reached for Carly's arm again.

She sidestepped him. "Who were you texting?"

"My boss."

"Why?"

"He'll send someone to your place. We need to speak with the police."

"I can't do that."

"Why not?"

"They threatened to take my son," she said, so quietly he almost didn't hear.

"The police?"

"No."

"Then who?" He knew he sounded impatient— because he felt impatient. He didn't play games, didn't keep secrets. He was a straight shooter and honest, almost to a fault.

"If I knew that, I'd have called the police the first time I was contacted." She started moving again. In the wrong direction. Heading for her vehicle, he assumed.

"We need to talk to the police," he repeated, not following her, because he knew she wouldn't go far. She needed his help more than she probably needed just about anything. She'd admitted as much when she'd given him her address.

She made it about a hundred feet before she stopped, turning around to face him, her dark ponytail swinging in a wide arc as she moved. "If they find out I've gone to the police, they'll take my son. I'll never see him again."

"Is that what they told you?"

"Yes."

"They'll have to get through some very well-trained people to get to him, Carly. Come on." He held out his hand and was surprised when she moved toward him. "We'll talk to the police, and then I'll bring you home."

"I can bring myself home," she muttered, but she'd reached his side, her eyes vibrant green against her tan skin. He could see that clearly now. Just like he could see that her running vest was navy blue rather than black. The world was waking, the sun bringing color to life—light brown grass, gray-black pavement, and the dark brown freckles on Carly's cheeks, threads of red and gold in her dark hair. She tucked a loose strand back into her ponytail holder, white scars crisscrossing a couple of her knuckles, her fingernails short and chipped. She worked with her hands, he'd guess, but he wasn't sure what kind of manual labor would afford her a place in a posh neighborhood in DC.

"What's your friend's name?" he asked, wondering if she lived with a boyfriend who paid the bills. It wasn't a very nice thought but was more in line with what he'd have expected from any of the girls Josh had dated when he'd lived at home.

"Jazz," she responded.

"He play in a band or something?"

"*She* is an author. Jasmine Rothschild. We went to

college together. She moved in after Zane was born, because I needed the help and she needed a place to stay."

"You said your son is six?"

"Yeah."

The twins would have been nearly seven.

If Zane was his nephew, there was a very real possibility that Lila and Carly had been pregnant at the same time. He wasn't sure how he felt about that, wasn't even sure he was supposed to feel anything. It sure didn't change what had happened.

He scowled, his knee aching as he walked. They weren't far from the neighborhood, but the woods were thick on either side of them, the dawn light only deepening the shadows of the forest. They'd walked past the same trees a few minutes ago, and he'd felt nothing. Not even a twinge of nerves. Now the woods had gone silent. No chipmunks or squirrels or tiny birds flitting from tree to tree. The breeze had stopped and the leaves weren't rustling, but somewhere in the deepest part of the shadows, a twig snapped.

He grabbed Carly's hand, feeling thick calluses on her fingertips but silky skin on her palms.

She didn't jerk back, didn't attempt to pull away.

"What is it?" she whispered as he dragged her off the path and tugged her down into thick undergrowth.

He leaned close, whispering in her ear, "Stay down and stay quiet."

She didn't respond, and he took that as agreement.

Someone was out there with them. And not the police. They'd have announced themselves by now.

He shifted, easing out from behind the brush and scanning the area. Staying low because, as far as he knew, the guy was still out there and still armed. Hopefully, he'd be too afraid to fire a shot and risk attracting police attention.

A phone buzzed, the sound a discordant note in the eerie silence.

He turned, gesturing for Carly to turn the thing off. She had it in her hand, was staring at the screen, her face leached of color.

"We need to go," she said, jumping up and trying to dart past him.

"I don't think so," he muttered, but there was something about her expression, the tension in her face, in her muscles, that made him snatch the phone from her hand and glance at the text she'd opened, the photo it contained. A white wicker table and chairs, bright red mums near a back door. A kid staring out from behind a window, his dark curly hair a lot like Carly's, his eyes...

Pale blue. Just like Josh's had been.

Dallas's pulse jumped, his mind racing with the possibility that Carly was telling the truth, that Zane really was his nephew.

She snatched the phone back, tucking it into her vest pocket, her hands shaking.

"They're going to take Zane. I'll never see him again," she said, her voice trembling.

"No. They aren't."

"They're outside my house, watching him."

"So are my coworkers," he responded, the hair on his nape standing on end, his skin crawling. A warning that he needed to heed. Someone was watching them. Someone was watching Zane. Someone who was very clearly trying to manipulate Carly.

They could go back and talk to the police. They *should* go back and talk to the police, but getting to

Carly's place was suddenly just as important. Yeah, someone from HEART was already there, but Dallas wanted to get a closer look at Carly's son, see if his eyes really were the same color blue as Josh's.

"What are you involved in? Drugs? Organized crime?" he growled, stepping back onto the path, his Glock in hand. Let the perp see that. Let him think twice about attacking.

"I'd starve to death before I did something illegal to earn money," she responded, her tone just as harsh as his had been.

"Someone is stalking your house, taking photos of your son. Seems like a warning to me."

"It is, but not because I'm involved in something I shouldn't be."

"Then what do they want?" He started running again, heading away from the police, away from his house. She had to have parked in the west lot, five or six miles from his place. A long run, but she'd had her agenda.

Now he had his. He wanted to meet Zane. He wanted to look in the boy's eyes, see if Josh was reflected there.

"They want me to use old-school techniques to create polished stones out of rough-cut gems." She was panting, running hard to keep pace with him, and he wasn't sure he'd heard her right.

"They want you to cut gemstones?"

"Yes."

"Because?"

"It's what I do. I'm a museum conservator, and I specialize in restoring antique jewelry. I'm one of a handful of people in North America who know and use Victorian- and Georgian-era stone-cutting methods."

That explained her scars and calluses. It didn't explain why someone was taking photos of her son.

"And?"

"Someone wants me to make replicas of some gemstones in a collection I've been working on for the Smithsonian."

"That isn't necessarily illegal."

"Not if they want replicas for personal enjoyment, but if that's what these people want, then why not just pay me to do it?"

"I'm assuming you've thought of a few answers to that."

"There's only one answer, Dallas. They're going to replace the originals. The gemstones I'm cutting are worth a tenth of what the originals are. On average, we're talking the difference between five and fifty thousand dollars. If they've gotten a metalworker to make facsimiles of the original settings, they'll be replacing fourteen pieces of jewelry worth one point five million dollars with forgeries."

"Seems like a lot of trouble to go through to get you to cooperate. It might have been easier to find someone willing to do the job for a price."

"There are only a few people in North America who can do what I do with enough expertise to make new cuts look old."

They'd reached the west entrance of the park, still running hard, his knee throbbing in protest, the muscle in his thigh cramping. He didn't slow his pace, though. Carly was heading for a black minivan parked beneath a streetlight. It looked like a family vehicle, the kind of thing suburbanites everywhere drove.

She unlocked the doors, jumping into the driver's

seat and starting the engine before he got his door open.
He jumped in and yanked it closed as she took off.

Maybe she'd hoped to leave him behind.

But even if she could have, he'd have found her again.
The story she'd told was interesting, and maybe it was
true.

He'd find out, and while he was at it, he'd get a good
look at the kid in the window, because sometimes pictures lied, sometimes memories did—and sometimes
what a person wanted to believe made him see things
that weren't really there.

THREE

She was terrified. More than she'd ever been.

They were there. At her house. Nothing but brick and mortar and glass separating them from Zane. It was easy enough to kick in a door, shatter a window, subdue a woman, leave with a little boy. How many stories had she heard of kids being snatched out of their beds? Most of them didn't end well.

Her hands tightened on the steering wheel, her heart thundering in her chest as she sped along the interstate. The exit was up ahead, and she took it too quickly, the back of the van shimmying, the tires squealing.

"Take it easy," Dallas said.

"I need to get to my son," she responded, surprised that her voice wasn't shaking, that she sounded calm. Years of practicing the art of self-control was paying off, her childhood need to distance herself from chaos, strife and drama creating a habit that was serving her well.

Too bad it wasn't doing anything for Zane. Or for Jazz. She'd fight to the death to keep Zane safe.

Carly shuddered, her stomach churning.

"It's going to be okay," Dallas said, and he sounded

so confident, so certain, that she would have believed him if she hadn't seen the photo, if she didn't know that the men who'd been threatening to take Zane were right outside her brownstone.

Had the photographer been standing in the backyard? Had Zane seen him?

She should have put more than bolts on the front and back doors. Should have changed out the old windows and replaced them with ones that had more secure locks.

She should have packed her things and run the day she'd gotten the first photo, the first phone call, the first threat. She'd thought she had it all under control. She'd been wrong. Which seemed to be the story of her life, the Achilles' heel that brought her down time and time again.

God had the perfect plan, the perfect timing, the unerring knowledge of everything that had been and would be. All she had to do was let Him guide her.

She'd heard that dozens of times from dozens of well-meaning friends at the dozens of churches she'd attended over the years. She'd chosen to attend church because it had been the one constant she could offer Zane, and because Jazz had insisted they start going.

Jazz had faith.

Jazz had joy.

Jazz had the kind of unfaltering optimism that would have driven Carly crazy if she hadn't loved her so much.

Carly had realism, skepticism and a healthy respect for the God of the universe.

He was there. She'd seen His handiwork too many times to ignore it.

She hit a red light at the first intersection in the

neighborhood, thought about blowing through it. She probably would have, but Dallas spoke again. "Don't."

That was it. One word that said he knew exactly what she was considering. He was right. Killing herself or someone else wouldn't solve her problems. Getting stopped by the police wouldn't help, either.

She braked too hard, her shaking leg refusing to co-operate with her brain.

"Sorry," she muttered, feeling the weight of his gaze, knowing that he was watching her.

She didn't want to meet his eyes. She didn't want to look into his face, but she couldn't stop herself. He was there. She was terrified. It was nearly full light, and she could see him clearly. He looked nothing like Josh. She wasn't sure why she was noticing or how it mattered, but Josh had been lean and hard, his face cut in steep angles and flat planes. Aside from his eyes, there'd been nothing remarkable about him. Nothing that had made women stop and look. It was his charm that had swept them off their feet.

And his lies.

Dallas was exactly the kind of man Carly imagined women noticed—tall, broad shouldered, well muscled. Handsome. He wore confidence like a cloak, and she couldn't help thinking that he looked like the kind of guy who could hold his own in a fight. He'd be a good ally and a daunting enemy.

She didn't want either of those things from him, though. She just needed his help. For now. Once Zane was safe, Dallas could go on with his life and she could go on with hers. No mess. No fuss.

Only, she wasn't sure he'd let that happen.

He hadn't known about Zane. His nephew. A connection to the brother he'd lost.

It was possible he'd want to keep in contact, be a part of Zane's life. Which would mean being part of her life. She didn't want that. Men were complications she'd removed from her life. It wasn't that she didn't sometimes wish Zane had a father to help usher him through childhood and into manhood. But she knew how terrible she was at differentiating good guys from bad ones. She knew how much drama, trauma and chaos the wrong guy could bring.

She'd lived it, and she wouldn't repeat it. Not ever.

She turned left into her neighborhood, her hands so tight on the steering wheel that her fingers were numb. Or maybe they were numb from fear.

Up ahead, a dark cloud swirled across the white-blue sky.

No. Not a cloud. Smoke. A plume of it, feathery tendrils wafting away as it rose.

A fire?

She eyed the dark gray smudge as she turned right, heading deeper into the residential area. A few mansions stood on oversize lots, the lawns manicured and pristine, the brick facades stately looking. A little farther in, mansions gave way to row homes. No shops or business. Just tall, narrow houses that had been neglected for decades and then brought back to life by savvy real estate investors.

Her brownstone was one of the smaller homes. Three bedrooms. Two bathrooms. A tiny kitchen with an eat-in area. It was an end unit, though, with plenty of natural light and a morning room that she used as a studio. That was where Zane had been this morning, staring out the window of her workroom, still dressed in the pajamas he'd worn to bed—the blue ones with red Corvettes zipping across the fabric.

He loved those pajamas. Just like he loved cars and trains and anything mechanical.

She didn't know where he'd gotten that from. Definitely not from her. She was into nature, the way light played across rocks and gemstones. She liked crafting things, creating something beautiful out of a dusty rough-cut gem.

The plume of smoke grew larger as she approached her street, the feathery tendrils darkening to charcoal. She could smell the fire—wood and rubber and electrical. A house fire. It had to be. And really close to her place.

Her heart jumped at the realization, her body going cold with it.

"No," she said, as if that could change things.

"What's wrong?" Dallas responded, but she couldn't speak, because she'd turned onto the one-way road that led home, and she could see flames jutting up into the smoke cloud, and she knew…knew before she could even see her pretty little brownstone, knew it was her place that was on fire.

They wanted Zane.

They were burning the house to get to him.

She stepped on the accelerator, running a stop sign, the horrible acrid scent of smoke permeating the van, filling her nose, stealing her breath.

"Calm down," Dallas commanded, his sharp tone pulling her back from the edge of panic.

"It's my house," she said.

"It could be anything, Carly."

"It could be, but it's not. It's my place. They're going to burn them out of the house. They may have already done it. Zane…"

She didn't finish, because the end of the street was in sight, her house and the narrow lot it sat on suddenly visible. Flames leaped from the front door, smoke swirling beneath the portico and up into the sky.

"Zane! Jazz!" she tried to shout, but the names came out as a whisper.

A few neighbors were outside, standing on the sidewalk and speaking into cell phones. They'd called for help, so she didn't waste time pulling out her phone. She threw the van into Park and jumped out, running toward the house, Dallas's shouted order to stop ringing hollowly in her ears as she bounded around the side of the building and headed for the backyard.

If he'd had his car, he'd have pulled out the fire extinguisher and put out the flames.

As bad as the smoke seemed, the fire was small, the flames shooting up from what looked like a pile of rags. Dallas noted that in passing, just like he noted two men standing a couple of hundred feet away, cell phones in their hands, eyes trained on the brownstone.

Neighbors?

He followed Carly around the house and through a white picket gate that led into the backyard. Like all the brownstones in the area, it had limited green space, the long yard twenty feet wide and dotted with scraggly winter grass.

A stone patio stood near an open sliding glass door.

Carly had already reached it when he grabbed her arm, pulling her back before she could enter the house.

"Stay here. I'll go in," he said, but she shook her head, her eyes wild with fear.

"They should be out already. Jazz would never stay in the house when there was a fire."

"If they're out, we don't need to go in," he responded as she tried to jerk her arm away.

"Something is wrong."

"You going in there won't make it right." He could hear sirens as the first responders sped their way. "Go around front and meet the fire crew. Let them know how many people are missing."

It was an order, and he expected her to obey it. Clients who didn't follow directions were a risk he couldn't take.

He released her arm and stepped into the house. The lower level of the townhome was large, the room he was standing in narrow but long and set up with comfortable furniture and a coffee table that looked nearly as old as the scuffed floor it was resting on. The kitchen was in front of him, open and spacious. A formal dining room stood just beyond that, and then a wall with partially closed pocket doors. It looked haphazard compared to the neatness of everything else, and he thought Jazz might have tried to close it as she and Zane were fleeing.

To keep the smoke out? The fire from spreading?

Or to stop someone from following?

There was a door to the right of the family room, and he headed for it, glancing into a workshop that had tables, tools, desk lamps. Shelves and tall chests of drawers that probably contained the tools of Carly's trade stood against the walls.

No closet. No place for anyone to hide, and he turned back to the family room and kitchen, stepping through the dining area with its old table and spindle chairs. Photos hung on the walls—pictures of Carly's life, her family, the things that she loved. He didn't have time for more than a glance; he could smell the fire and smoke, see tendrils of black through the open pocket doors. He pushed them farther apart, walking into a living room that was as neat and orderly as the rest of the house. No toys. No clutter. The furniture was modern and bright. A Christmas tree stood near the front windows. Small and potted, one of those living trees that people planted once Christmas ended.

Smog-thick smoke hung in the air, the room tinged with gray-black. The front door was intact, the varnished wood staircase leading upstairs untouched. He headed up, knowing that Carly was behind him. He could hear her feet pounding on the wood floor, the rustle of her clothes in the quiet house. The muted scream of sirens was the only other sound.

It was unnaturally quiet. His body hummed with adrenaline.

He reached the landing, the rising smoke heavier there, and jogged the rest of the way up, ignoring the photos that lined the wall, because every one of them contained an imagine of Zane. It was obvious the kid was loved and happy, that he had the kind of life every child deserved. The kind of life Dallas had planned to give his children. The kind he'd never had. It was obvious Carly had been doing everything she could to provide a safe environment for him to grow and flourish.

And now this had happened. Something ugly and mean and dangerous had come into their lives. Whether or not Zane was really his nephew didn't matter nearly as much as making sure he was okay.

"Zane! Jazz!" Carly called, her voice echoing through the narrow hallway as she ran up the stairs.

"If they're here, they're being quiet," he responded, glancing into a bedroom at the top of the steps. Blue walls and white wainscoting, a twin bed with a light blue comforter. Toy box. Cars in a line on the floor near the bed.

"Zane! Jazz!" she repeated, running past him.

He thought she planned to look in the other rooms. The house was quiet. There was no sign of either of the people who should have been there. They could have escaped. They could have been kidnapped.

They could be in the house and unable to respond.

He could think of more than one reason why that might be the case. None of them good.

He followed Carly to the next room, watching as she opened an armoire, peered under a four-poster bed, ran to an attached bathroom and yanked open the shower curtain.

When she tried to leave the room, he blocked her path.

"I told you to meet the first responders and let them know how many people are missing." He spoke conversationally, easily, as if there wasn't a fire burning on the front porch, filling the house with smoke. As if her friend and son weren't missing. As if they were reasonable people in a reasonable situation.

He wasn't reasonable. Not when it came to his work. There was a way to do things, and there was a way to mess things up.

"Move," she growled, her eyes flashing with anger and fear.

"You came to me," he reminded her. "You obviously

thought I had the expertise that could get you out of the mess you were in. Right?"

She pressed her lips together and didn't speak.

"I'll take your silence as agreement."

"I may need your help, but I don't need you to tell me what to do or how to do it." She tried to move past him, frowning when he didn't step aside. "My life would be easier if you'd move."

"Our relationship will be easier if you trust me."

"We don't have a relationship."

"Not yet, but if you're really the mother of my nephew, we will."

"Why would I lie?"

"Why would someone blackmail you into forging antique jewelry?" he replied.

She frowned, her eyes dark with fatigue and concern. "Greed? Desperation? There are probably a dozen other possible reasons."

"Exactly. People do a lot of unconscionable things for reasons that only make sense to them."

"And?"

"Most days, I like to check people out before I agree to help with their problems. I'm here anyway. How about you make my job easier and trust that I know what I'm doing?" He walked into the hall, letting her decide to follow or not. There were two people missing, and he didn't want to waste any more time chatting about how things should be. Either she'd cooperate, or she wouldn't. If she didn't, things would be more complicated but not impossible. He'd worked around plenty of difficult clients. In the end, things usually went the way he wanted.

To his surprise, she didn't follow him to the next

room. Instead, she ran back downstairs. He'd take that as a sign that she intended to do what he'd asked. Hopefully, it was also a sign that she was being honest about the situation she was in.

He pulled out his cell phone, dialing Chance's number as he surveyed the small bedroom. The double bed just fit, a small dresser squeezed in beside it. He opened a closet and looked inside. Empty. This must be the spare room. Like the rest of the house, it was pristine.

"What kind of trouble are you getting yourself into?" Chance's voice rang in his ear as he moved to the next room. "Boone and I just reached the address you gave, and there are fire trucks and police cars everywhere. We can't park anywhere near the house."

"Someone set a fire on the front stoop. Lots of smoke. Hopefully not a lot of damage."

"That doesn't answer my question. What kind of trouble are you in?"

"I'm not in trouble. My sister-in-law is."

"The one you haven't met or spoken to *ever*?" Chance asked, because he knew just about everything there was to know about every member of HEART. That was the way he ran his business. Every employee knew it, and no one complained. They understood the job—the inherent risks, the emotional toll. They also understood as much about Chance as he did about them. He cared deeply about the men and women who worked for him. He never asked any of them to do something he wouldn't, and he always had their backs. On the job or off it.

That kind leadership bred loyalty and there wasn't a member of HEART who wouldn't do anything Chance asked.

"That would be the one," Dallas responded as he walked into a third room. "She should be coming around to the front of the house. Dark hair in a ponytail, running gear."

"I've got her," Chance said. "She's running toward a fire truck."

"Can you keep an eye on her? I'm inside. Looking for her son and friend."

Chance was silent for a moment, probably weighing the meaning behind the words, searching through the database in his head and trying to figure out if he'd ever heard anything about Dallas having a nephew.

"I'll keep any eye on her," he finally said.

"And I'll fill you in on the details after I finish searching the house. Thanks, Chance." He hung up, eyeing the interior of the room he'd just entered. It was different from the rest of the house. Eclectic. Not streamlined and free of clutter. There were shelves of books on the walls, an unmade bed, a pile of papers on an old secretary desk. A computer sat in the middle of the mess of pages, turned on, the screen blue. He rounded the bed, moving toward the desk and the small door to its left.

He saw the foot first—bare and pale—then the leg. Fuzzy pajama pants and dark pink T-shirt. A woman. Facedown. Blond hair cut short, blood seeping from a wound near her ear.

His heart jumped, and then he was kneeling beside her, feeling for a pulse with one hand while he called Chance, told him to send in the EMTs.

Pulse thready. Respiration shallow. Wound on the head, a deep cut and a huge knot that could have been caused by just about anything. He suspected metal. He suspected a gun.

Jazz Rothschild. It had to be her, and she was alone. No sign of Zane.

Footsteps pounded up the stairs, and he called out to let the emergency responders know his location. He didn't leave Jazz's side until they were in the room, crowding around her prone body. Destroying evidence, but he wasn't the person to point that out. He scanned the room, looking for hiding places that might conceal a six-year-old.

How big would that be? Forty pounds? More?

If the twins had lived, he'd know. He'd have seven years of experience to draw.

If…

He opened the closet, ignoring an EMT who asked him to step out of the room. Jazz had as colorful a wardrobe as she did a room. If he'd had to guess, he'd have said that she and Carly had opposite personalities and very different ways of looking at the world.

He checked under the bed, pulled back thick drapes that covered the windows, opened a brightly painted armoire that stood against the wall.

By the time he finished, the medical crew was carrying in a backboard, and he was getting desperate. Someone had attacked Jazz. That was obvious. It was also obvious that a six-year-old child was missing. He could be hiding somewhere or he could be in the hands of the person who'd been manipulating his mother. Either way, he needed to be found. He needed to be brought back safely. And the person responsible needed to be brought to justice.

FOUR

She was wading through mud.

That was how it felt, anyway.

Running and getting nowhere.

She'd seen the EMTs heading around the side of the
house, moving at a quick clip. She'd have followed immediately if she hadn't been answering the fire mar-
shal's questions.

Now she was free, all the questions answered, and
she couldn't get to the house fast enough.

She knew Dallas had found something. Found some-
one. Jazz or Zane or both. Injured. Maybe worse.

She couldn't shake the fear that was crawling along
her spine. She couldn't make herself stop thinking the
unthinkable and imagining the worst.

And she couldn't seem to run fast enough.

She finally reached the front of the house, the scent
of smoke heavy in the cold air. The fire had been extin-
guished, and there were a few firefighters snapping photos of the aftermath. The thick wood door was singed,
the cement stoop black with soot. She didn't look up
at the portico. She'd worry about that after she found
her family.

A cold breeze whipped through her running gear as she ran into the backyard. The sun had disappeared behind thick gray clouds, and it looked like a winter storm might be blowing in.

Zane loved rain and snow and ice. He loved winter and playing outside in the cold.

He loved life, and he trusted everyone. To him, the world was a glorious place filled with friendly people. She hadn't ever had the heart to tell him differently. Sure, she'd taught him stranger danger and to be cautious; she'd warned him about the tricks adults might use to lure him away. She'd rehearsed scenarios with him, role-playing so that he could practice running, fighting, screaming.

But it had all been a game to him, and she'd never been sure the lessons were getting through. The world could be an ugly place. She had learned that at a young age. She hadn't wanted Zane to have to do the same. She'd wanted him protected and sheltered and secure. She'd worked hard to make sure he had everything he needed and some of what he wanted. She paid for Montessori school so that he could be a free thinker, an individual. She'd done everything in her power to give him the life he deserved, but somehow, she'd still failed him.

She felt cold with the knowledge, sick with it.

She ran to the sliding glass door, darting past a police officer who was talking into a radio. He shouted something, but she kept going. The EMTs were somewhere on the second floor. She could hear their boots on the wood above her head. Jazz's room? Or hers?

She ran toward the front of the house and the staircase, her heart beating frantically.

"Ms. Kelley?" Someone touched her shoulder, and

she jumped, swinging around to face a tall, lean man dressed in black slacks and a white button-up shirt. He looked like a businessman. Or an FBI agent.

"Yes." She swung back around and would have kept running, but he touched her shoulder again.

"I'm Chance Miller."

"Okay." She didn't care who he was. She was going upstairs. She was going to see whatever was there. She was going to face this head-on just like she had faced everything else in her life. Only this time, she had a feeling that facing it was going to be the toughest thing she'd ever done. This time, she wasn't sure she'd survive it.

She couldn't lose Zane. She couldn't lose Jazz, either. They were all she had. Her only family.

"I work with Dallas. This is my coworker Boone Anderson," he continued, gesturing toward a man who seemed to appear out of nowhere. Redheaded, lean and very tall, he had the kind of boy-next-door look that automatically made you want to trust him.

"I'm sorry, I don't have time—"

"Do you ever play hide-and-seek with your son?" Chance cut her off, and she tried to wrap her mind around what he was asking, tried to make sense of the question.

"Hide-and-seek? Occasionally, but it's not a game we play often."

"So he doesn't have a special hiding place? A spot he always goes to when he's trying to trick you?" Boone spoke this time, his Southern drawl warm and thick, his smile kind.

She didn't want his kindness. She wanted her son, her

friend and the truth about what had happened to them. "Why are you asking me this? Did Dallas find Jazz?"

Neither responded, and that was answer enough.

She bolted, running up the stairs and down the hall.

Jazz's room was crowded with people. Carly shoved into the throng, saw her best friend lying on the floor, face chalk white, eyes closed, head bandaged. They'd put a brace around her neck and a blood-pressure cuff on her arm, but she was silent and still, unaware of the chaos around her.

"Jazz!" Carly knelt beside her, lifting her hand, relieved that it felt warm.

"Ma'am," an EMT said, "we're going to have to transport her to the hospital. She has a pretty serious head injury. You'll need to step out of the way so that we can move her onto the gurney."

She did as she was asked, because she didn't want to hold up the process. She'd known Jazz for nearly fifteen years, and in all that time, she had never known her to be silent. Even when she was writing, she was loud, mumbling under her breath as she created, talking to herself and anyone else who happened to be around. *Artistic, funny, sarcastic, loving, loyal.* Those were all words that described her well. *Quiet, still, restful* were not.

"What happened to her?" she asked, and the EMT shrugged.

"Near as we can tell, someone whacked her on the back of the head. Looks like she took the hit right behind her ear. It probably knocked her out instantly."

"How bad is it?"

"We won't know until she gets a CAT scan. If you could step out of the way…" He moved between her and

Jazz, and she had no choice but to take a step back, to see the entirety of the room, the laptop and papers and mug of coffee sitting on the nightstand near the bed.

There was a car beside one of the pillows. Matchbox size. Blue—Zane's favorite color.

"Has anyone seen my son?" she asked, but the EMTs were too busy coordinating their movements and shifting Jazz onto the backboard to hear. Or maybe they heard but had no answer.

"We're taking her to DC General. It's closest," the EMT said as he and his coworkers lifted Jazz and headed into the hall. Carly wanted to follow, to get in the ambulance and make sure Jazz was okay, but Zane was still missing.

Kidnapped?

Hurt?

Hiding?

She moved blindly, following the group until they started downstairs. She was frozen there, torn between her loyalty to her friend and her desperate need to find her son.

"I'll head to the hospital," someone said, and she glanced over her shoulder, saw Boone standing a few feet away. He was watching her with a mixture of sympathy and understanding. "Make sure she gets the treatment she needs. Anyone I should call?"

"Her fiancé. Brett Williams. His number is in her cell phone. That's in her handbag." Because, unlike most of the Western world, Jazz wasn't glued to her electronic devices. She used the phone to communicate, her laptop for email. Everything else she had was old-school and antiquated. It drove Brett crazy. Jazz had admitted that to Carly a few months ago. He wanted her plugged in all the time, easily accessible and quick to answer texts or phone calls.

Jazz had laughed while she'd told the story. Carly hadn't found it nearly as amusing. To her, it seemed that Brett was already trying to change Jazz, that he was more interested in making her into what he wanted her to be than accepting her for the woman she was.

"The handbag?" Boone prodded gently. "Where is it?"

"I think—"

"Right here?" Chance walked out of the bedroom, an oversize teal bag in his hand. Just like Jazz, it was loud and beautiful. Carly had bought it for her three Christmases ago, and Jazz never went anywhere without it.

"Yes. Thank you."

"Want to check it to make sure her phone, ID and insurance card are in it?"

She wanted to find her son. That was what she wanted. She wanted to go to the hospital and make sure Jazz was okay, too.

She wanted a lot of things. Digging through her friend's purse wasn't one of them, but she did it anyway, pulling out a Power Rangers figurine, a chocolate bar, a small bag of pretzels and, finally, Jazz's flip phone and wallet.

"They're here," she said.

"I'll contact her fiancé," Boone said, taking the phone, wallet and bag. "Your mobile number is in here, too?"

"Yes."

"I'll text when she regains consciousness, and I'll let you know what they find on the CAT scan."

"Thank you—" She'd been told his name. She knew that, but she couldn't remember it.

"Boone," he provided with the same kind smile he'd offered before. "Hopefully, you'll hear from me soon." He loped down the stairs, all long legs and lean muscles, and she turned blindly, walking to Zane's room, standing on the threshold.

He wasn't there. She knew that, but she wanted him to be. She wanted to lift the edge of his comforter, look under the bed and find him. She wanted him to jump out of the closet and scream *boo!* Or step out from behind the thick curtains that were pulled across the windows.

"Zane!" she called, her voice echoing in the silent room.

She thought she heard a faint response. It had to be her imagination, but she called again, stepping out into the hall, ignoring Chance's questioning look.

"Zane!" She cocked her head to the side, listening but hearing nothing.

"Zane!" She stepped back into his room and heard the faint whisper again. This time she was sure it was his voice calling for her.

"Where are you?" she shouted, her heart racing, her pulse pounding in her ears.

This time, the room was silent.

"Dallas checked all the rooms on this level and the one above it. He's up in the attic now." Chance glanced at his cell phone and frowned. "Says he thought he heard something, but when he called Zane, he got no response. Maybe he heard you?"

"Maybe." Or maybe all those lessons on stranger danger had paid off. Maybe instead of making friends with the guys who'd set the fire, Zane had run from them. She walked up to the third floor. Like the one below it, this level had three rooms. They used one as a guest room. The larger of the remaining two was Jazz's studio. Zane's playroom was right beside it. Jazz had insisted on having a connecting door put in between the two spaces, and when Zane wasn't in school, they spent hours moving between the two rooms.

Carly walked into the playroom and across the scuffed wood floor. Zane's toys were put away, his books stacked neatly on shelves. On the far wall, a narrow door led to the attic stairs. Usually it was locked, but Dallas must have found the key. Wouldn't be difficult, since it was hanging from a hook beside the door.

Or that was where it should have been.

It was missing. Dallas must have brought it with him.

Carly ran up the stairs, the boards creaking and groaning under her feet. Gray light streamed in from the large dormer windows on the east side of the house. Three smaller windows were to the west. It was a spacious and bright area that she could have used for her workroom if it hadn't been so filled with other people's abandoned stuff. She hadn't had time to change that. Eventually, though, she would. She loved her workroom, but this space had natural light and plenty of square footage. She could set up a study area for Zane in one corner and a work space for herself in another, and there'd still be plenty of room.

"Dallas?" she called, knowing he was up here but not certain where.

"Behind the boxes near the east dormer," he responded, his voice muffled.

She followed the sound, pressing between stacks

of boxes and finding her way into a cleared area near the wall.

Dallas was a few feet away, crouching near what looked like a small door made of paneling. Even bent low, he looked large, his broad shoulders nearly blocking her view of the panel door.

Nothing at all like his brother.

But, then, they'd been half siblings.

Same mother. Different fathers.

At least, that was what Josh had told her.

Maybe, for once, he'd told the truth.

"Where does this lead?" Dallas asked, touching the panel, his broad palm sliding against the dark wood.

"I don't know. I've never seen it before. Probably nowhere. This place is old. A lot has changed since it was first built."

"Someone has seen it before, and I'm almost certain the panel has been opened recently. There's no dust near it or on it." He ran his hand across the floor, showed her his clean fingers.

"You don't think Zane is in there?"

"I heard someone calling from behind the panel." He rapped his fist against the wood.

"I was in Zane's room, calling for him," she offered. "You might have heard that."

"I don't think so," he responded, and her pulse jumped. Hope. That was what it felt like.

"Zane?" she called, leaning closer to the panel, searching for a knob or button. Anything to make it open.

"Did you try sliding it up?" Chance asked as he eased into the small space, his shoulder bumping Carly's. She moved in response, sliding another couple of inches in Dallas's direction. They were arm to arm now, and she could feel the firmness of his muscles beneath his coat, feel the heat of his body filling the small area. It reminded her of the early days of her relationship with Josh, how comforting it had felt to be around him, how nice to know she wasn't alone. She hadn't known about his lies, his deception, his selfishness then; she'd only known the way he'd made her laugh and helped her carry her books back to her dorm room.

She'd been young and naive and desperate for something she should have known she would never have.

She'd matured a lot since then. She'd learned a lot about herself and what she wanted.

Peace.

That was the beginning and the end of it. No drama. No lies. No tears or anger or harsh words. Just her people—Jazz and Zane—living easily together.

"I tried sliding it up," Dallas said. "Tried sliding it sideways. I tried pushing it in. It doesn't budge. Something is moving around in there, though. Listen."

The attic went silent, and Carly could hear it—a muffled rustling, a soft tap.

"A rat?" Chance suggested, and Carly backed up, bumped a pile of boxes and sent them toppling.

Behind the panel, something thumped loudly enough to make her jump.

Not a rat. It was too big.

But not Zane, either. He was a good kid, a rule follower, compliant in a way she'd never been. He liked routine and order and clear directions.

"It can't be Zane. He's not allowed in the attic by himself," she said. "We keep it locked, and he's not supposed to touch the key."

"It was unlocked when I got here. That's why I came up," Dallas said, standing up and reaching as far as he could toward the ceiling, sliding his palms along a support beam and frowning. "Nothing there."

"If we can't figure out how to get in there, I don't see how my six-year-old son could." But that thing that felt like hope was coming to life in her, chasing away some of the fear, making her lean in close to the paneling and shout through the old wood, "Zane! Can you hear me? It's Mom!"

This time, she heard the response clearly—the faint cry of a child, three hard raps on the wall near her head.

She met Dallas's eyes.

"He's in there," she said, surprised, relieved, terrified.

What if they couldn't get him out? What if another fire was set and he was trapped? What if—

"Whatever you're thinking," Dallas said, meeting her eyes, "stop. He's fine. We'll get him out, and we'll figure out how he got there in the first place." He leaned close to the panel door and shouted, "Can you open the door, Zane?"

"Aunt Jazz always does. She said to close the panel once I got in. So I did."

"Your aunt isn't here. Can you do it this time?"

"I tried, but it's stuck. Plus, I was only supposed to close the panel. I forgot, and I closed the door, too." Zane must have moved closer. His words were clearer, and Carly could tell that he'd been crying.

"It's okay, sweetie. We'll have you out in no time." Knowing Jazz, she'd explored every inch of the attic while Zane was at school, discovered the secret room and made it their thing—hers and Zane's. Which would be fine, except now Carly had no idea how to rescue her son.

"How did you get in there?" Dallas asked.

"The button opens the panel, and the door is behind it. I turned the key and came in. Just like Jazz showed me."

"Where's the button?" Chance asked.

"On the wood at the top of the stairs," Zane responded, finally offering the information they needed.

The right questions produced the right answers. Just like the right cut produced the right facet.

She stood, but Chance was already crossing the large space and studying the wood near the stairway.

"I don't see anything," he said.

"Where exactly is it, Zane Timothy?" she yelled, and she felt Dallas tense, his muscles suddenly taut, his body still.

"On the big post! In the flower."

"Honey, there are no flowers on the big..." Her voice trailed off as the panel slid sideways, revealing the bottom two-thirds of a door. Old, dingy white with a skeleton key hanging from a loop of yarn that someone had hooked over the crystal doorknob.

Teal yarn. Jazz had left a little piece of herself there.

Dallas unlocked the door. "Step away from the door, Zane. I'm opening it," he called and then pushed inward, old hinges creaking, cold air wafting out as the cavity beyond was revealed.

Zane didn't have to be coerced out of hiding.

He ran, his skinny body making a beeline for his mother. Dallas watched as his scrawny arms locked around her waist, his hands fisted in her jacket. He had a

dark smudge on one cheek, tear streaks on both, and he
was shaking with cold, the thin footy pajamas he wore
no match for the frigid air that seeped from the room.
He could have frozen in there. Whatever the room had
been meant for, it wasn't insulated. Dallas slid out of
his jacket and tucked it around Zane's narrow shoulders
before he ducked into the small opening.

The room was dimly lit, a small window about three
feet from the floor letting in grayish light. Bare wood
floor, unvarnished and splintering. The walls were nothing but solid support beams and exterior brick. He could
hear the wind gusting and feel it blowing through dozens of slivery cracks in the facade. A blanket lay near
the door, and a small table had been set up near the
interior wall. Little plates and cups sat on top of it.
Books were piled on the floor beside it. A small fake
tree stood in the corner, a gift wrapped in shiny red
paper beneath it.

"Why did Aunt Jazz tell you to come up here, Zane?"
Carly asked, her voice muted even with the door open.
She hadn't looked into the small room. She was too
busy hugging her son.

He didn't blame her.

He'd have been doing the same.

"Smoke was coming in the house, so Aunt Jazz said
we had to go out the back door. But when I opened it, a
man was there. He tried to grab me, so Aunt Jazz beat
him up. Like this."

Dallas ducked back out of the room just in time to
see Zane throwing a weak right hook, thumbs tucked
into his fingers.

It made him smile.

It also made him worry.

Zane was only six, and he looked small for his age. He'd be no match for anyone who meant him harm.

"Looks like your aunt did a good job protecting you," Dallas said, meeting Chance's eyes. No doubt, they were thinking the same thing: a vulnerable child who needed protection.

The team knew how to handle that. They knew exactly how to keep anyone safe. As long as the person they were protecting was willing to cooperate.

He glanced at Carly.

She was watching her son, her jaw tight, her face leached of color. "Did you see the man at the door?" she asked quietly.

Zane shrugged. "Aunt Jazz told me to run to our special place. So, I did."

"Good for you, Zane. I'm proud of how you handled this." Carly's voice was shaking, but she'd pasted a smile on her face.

"Where's Aunt Jazz? She'll be proud, too!"

"She's…at the hospital. She hurt her head, and the doctors are making sure she's okay."

"We better go there. She'll be scared if she's by herself. I'll get dressed, and we can go." He handed Dallas his coat and darted away, running down the attic stairs.

Carly darted after him, her ponytail bouncing against her back.

"I guess we're going to handle this?" Chance said before Dallas could follow.

"I'm still on medical leave," Dallas responded, already moving down the stairs.

"That wasn't the question."

"I'm going to handle it." He jogged down to the third

floor, the sound of a high-pitched kid's voice drifting from somewhere ahead.

Singing.

Amazing Grace.

"Then the team will handle it, too. That's how it works. I'll go down and talk to the police. They'll want to interview Zane. We'll see if that can happen at the hospital. You keep an eye on the kid. If there's a problem, let me know."

They'd reached the second floor.

Carly was standing outside Zane's door, forehead against the polished wood, ponytail snaking down the middle of her back. She could have been praying or crying, her narrow shoulders tense, her muscles taut.

He knew her fear. He'd felt it, and if he'd known her better, he'd have put a hand on her shoulder and told her everything would be okay.

On the other side of the door, Zane was still singing, the last note of every stanza warbling for a few seconds too long.

"He doesn't seem any worse for wear," he said, and Carly jumped, whirling around to face him.

Her eyes were dry.

No tears.

Just a hint of anger flashing from their depths.

"He's like that all the time," Carly commented as if Dallas had asked a question she needed to answer. "Always happy and singing and carefree. Everyone who meets him loves him."

"My brother was like that when he was little. Very charming and sweet. If he'd had the right beginning…" He didn't finish. There was no sense in it. Josh had been born addicted to drugs. Therapists had concluded that his brain had been damaged from that. Dallas thought his brain had been damaged by an addict mother and dozens of druggies who were in and out of the house at all times of the day and night.

"He was charming and sweet when we met. I guess he knew how to access that part of himself." She knocked on the door, a quick, soft rap that did nothing to stop Zane's singing.

"Sweetheart, you need to hurry. I want to go to the hospital to see how Aunt Jazz is doing," she said patiently.

"I'm done!" Zane responded. The door flew open, and he was there dressed from head to toe in Spider-Man gear.

"Let's go!" He grabbed Carly's hand and tugged her toward the stairs, probably rushing in the hopes that she wouldn't notice his outfit. A choice that—despite the situation—made Dallas smile.

"Not until you put some shoes on," Carly responded, stopping at the top of the stairs and looking into her son's face. "Boots are a better idea. It looks like it might snow. Grab your heavy coat and mittens." She sounded like every mother—a mixture of patient exasperation and love.

"But, Mom, if I wear those, no one will see that I'm a superhero."

"I'm sure people will see," she responded with a wry smile.

"I want the bad guy to see. I want him to know he can't get me or you or Aunt Jazzy!" But Zane ran to his room anyway, returning moments later with his feet shoved in dark blue snow boots, his outfit covered with a thick down coat. He was pulling his hands into mittens as he ran down the stairs, Carly right on his heels.

She didn't invite Dallas to follow. He did anyway.

If she was going to the hospital, he was, too, whether she wanted the company or not. Whether she thought she needed his help, wanted his help, regretted asking for his help, didn't matter. What mattered was that Dallas had looked in Zane's eyes, and he'd seen his brother there.

There could be no turning away from that, no forgetting it.

Dallas had never been able to help Josh. Nothing he'd ever done or said had changed the course of his brother's life.

But he could keep his child safe. He could be part of Zane's life. He could introduce him to his grandparents, let him know that he had more than just his mother and his aunt to count on. Family was important.

First, though, Dallas had to find the people who were after Zane, put a stop to whatever forgery operation they were running and throw them in jail with the rest of the scumbags he'd stopped over the years.

A life with purpose. That was what he'd wanted to achieve. But it might just be that he needed more. That he needed something to focus on besides his work and his empty house.

Maybe all the words he'd whispered to God in the middle of the longest nights had been heard, all his angry ranting and accusations, his disgust at the fact that he'd been spared and his family taken, had resulted in this. Maybe meeting his nephew would change his focus, help him figure out exactly what he was missing and why he missed it.

Or maybe it was just another opportunity to help someone who needed it.

Either way, Dallas wouldn't let Carly and Zane walk away. Not until he knew for certain they'd be safe.

FIVE

She'd opened Pandora's box and released something unexpected.

Carly couldn't decide whether it was a good or a bad thing.

Right now, it seemed good. It would continue to seem good as long as there were people who wanted to kidnap Zane.

She wasn't sure how it would seem when the danger was over.

She'd been convinced Josh's family knew that he'd been expecting a child. The fact that none of them had come to the funeral, that they hadn't called, that there'd been no effort to reach out and find out if the baby had been born, had seemed to prove that they didn't care.

That had been fine with her. She knew she could support herself and a child. She didn't need Josh's family, and she hadn't spent much time thinking about them or wondering if they wanted to know that they had a grandson. She'd been too busy, too distracted by motherhood and work, by moving from place to place for contracted jobs at museums all over the country. She hadn't had spare time to think about Zane's extended family—

the uncle he didn't know, the grandparents who hadn't seemed to care that he existed.

They hadn't cared because they hadn't known. That seemed obvious now that she'd met Dallas, seen the way he'd looked at her son, studied his face, searched for pieces of his brother there. He obviously cared, and if he told his parents, they might care, too.

They might want to meet Zane, be part of his life. She wasn't sure how she felt about that.

She grabbed her winter coat from the closet near the front door. One-handed, because her other hand was on Zane's shoulder, holding him in place. She didn't want him going anywhere without her.

She didn't plan to let him out of her sight. Not today. Not tomorrow. Not a week from now. Which she knew was totally unreasonable and impossible, but it was how she felt.

He could have been kidnapped. He could have frozen to death in the little room in the attic. Anything could have happened and probably would have if they'd arrived at the house a few minutes later.

"It would be easier to put that on if you let go of your son," Dallas said, taking the coat from her hand and holding it while she shoved one arm in.

"If I have to let go to put the coat on, maybe I don't need one after all," she responded, and he chuckled.

"You can't superglue him to you, Carly, so you may as well get the thought out of your head."

"We have superglue," Zane offered as Carly finally released her grip on his shoulder. "But Mom says it's not for kids."

"Your mom is right." Dallas was doing it again, studying Zane's face. There was no doubt he could see his brother in Zane's eyes, in the turn of his nose, in his bowed upper lip. Zane was a couple of shades darker than his father had been—none of the pale Irish Kelley genes—but he had a few freckles on his cheeks and a dimple in his chin.

"She usually is," Zane said, and Dallas laughed.

"You're a smart young man."

"That's what my teachers say, but I think they just like me." Zane offered a quick smile, but he seemed to be studying Dallas the same way Dallas had studied him. "Who are you?"

"I'm—" He glanced at Carly, letting her make the decision about how they would be introduced.

"Remember I told you that your father had one brother?" she said. She wouldn't hide the truth because that wouldn't be fair to either of them. "This is his brother."

"Oh. What's his name?" Zane didn't look surprised, he didn't look intrigued, he just looked like his normal self—happy and excited by life.

"Dallas."

"Like the city in Texas?"

"You really are smart, kid," Dallas said, and Zane's smile broadened.

"Aunt Jazz wrote a book about all the states. She gave me a copy, and I read it a lot. Want to see?"

"Sure. After we go visit her at the hospital."

"Did the bad guy hurt her?"

"We're not sure what happened," Carly said quickly. That was the truth, too, and Zane seemed satisfied with it. Which was good, because she didn't want to give him unnecessary details.

"That bad guy probably did hurt her, but I think she

hurt him worse. She punched him right in the nose." He swung a quick right hook. "She's pretty tough. Right, Mom?"

He seemed to need reassurance, so she nodded, her throat tight with emotions she wasn't going to let him see. Relief because he was okay. Worry for Jazz. Fear for both of them.

This wasn't over.

It wouldn't be over until they found the people who'd been blackmailing her and threw them in jail.

She didn't know how many people were involved. She didn't know how much money they'd invested, but she knew they meant business. If she'd had any doubts before, she didn't now.

"She's going to be happy to see you, Spidey," Dallas said, his gaze on Carly.

There were questions in his green-blue eyes, but he didn't voice them. She was glad, because there were only so many answers she could give in front of Zane.

"I know, and she'll love my outfit!" Zane agreed enthusiastically, reaching for the front doorknob.

"Hold on, sweetie." Carly pulled him away. "We'll go out the back."

"We never go out the back."

"Today we will, because there was a fire on the front stoop, and it's still a mess. We don't want to track black soot through the hospital."

"That's right." Zane nodded sagely. "I forgot about all that smoke, but I've been thinking…"

"What?"

"What if the bad guy is still out back? What if he's waiting for us to walk outside? Just like before?"

"The police are out there, and the firefighters.

They'll chase any bad guys away," she responded, trying to keep her voice light and unaffected, her expression neutral. He was scared, and she didn't blame him, but if he saw that she was, too, that would make things a hundred times worse for him.

"And I'm here," Dallas said, crouching so he and Zane were eye to eye. "I won't let anything happen to you."

"I'm not worried about me. I'm worried about Mom. She can't fight like Aunt Jazz. She doesn't have the karate moves."

"I won't let anything happen to her, either," he said, a hint of a smile on his face.

"Promise?"

"Promise."

Don't do that, she wanted to say. *Don't promise him things that you might not be able to follow through on.*

That was what her entire childhood had been. Broken promises. One right after another.

So far, her adulthood hadn't been much better.

When she'd had Zane, when she'd looked into his tiny wrinkled face for the first time, she'd vowed that she would always follow through, that she would never offer him something she didn't intend to give.

But Dallas's promise seemed to make Zane happy. He bounced away from the front door, heading toward the back of the house. He stopped at the yellow caution tape that was strung between the kitchen and family room. Several people in white jumpsuits were kneeling on the floor, taking pictures and putting markers near what looked like splotches of blood.

She hadn't noticed them before. She'd been too anxious, too focused on finding Zane and Jazz.

"Wow!" Zane breathed, and one of the people glanced their way. A woman, her hair covered with a white hood, her red lipstick almost garish against her pale skin. Carly thought she'd tell them to stay on their side of the line, but she straightened and walked toward them, her stride brisk, her expression hard.

"Is this the witness?" she said without introducing herself.

"That depends on who wants to know," Dallas responded before Carly could.

The woman frowned. "I'm Sergeant Bliss Wright. Chance Miller and I go way back. You're Dallas Morgan?"

"That's right."

"And you must be Zane." She smiled, her expression softening.

"That's right," he responded, mimicking Dallas.

"I thought I'd come to the hospital in a little while and ask you a few questions while I'm there. Does that sound okay?"

"You should be asking me that question," Carly cut in. "He's a little young to understand what this is all about."

"I understand," Zane argued. "I've seen this on those cop shows Aunt Jazz likes to watch. They always question the witness right after, because that's when the memory is best. Sometimes, they question them a lot of times, and they even go to the police station. Are we going there?"

"Would you rather do it there?"

"No!" Carly nearly shouted, and everyone in the room turned to look.

She felt like a fool, her cheeks hot, her pulse racing, but she was still afraid of saying too much to the police.

She'd been warned a dozen times in a dozen ways to keep her mouth shut. She'd done it because she'd been afraid for Zane. She was still afraid.

"What I mean is, the hospital is fine. You can interview him there. If I can be present."

"That won't be a problem. I'd like to interview you, as well. How about we meet in an hour? I'm waiting for the evidence team to arrive. Once they do, I'll head over to the hospital. Do you have a business card with your cell phone number? I can call when I get there."

"I have one, but not on me."

"Here's mine." Dallas fished a card out of his wallet and handed it to the sergeant. It felt a little too much like he was taking control, stepping in and fixing what Carly could have fixed herself. She almost insisted on going out to the van, grabbing her purse and getting a business card from it.

But she'd wanted Dallas's help. She'd spent weeks planning a way to get it.

Either she could step out of the way and let him do what he did best, or she could put up roadblocks and make everything more difficult. Her younger self would have gone with the latter option, but she'd matured a lot in the past six years. She could look at the big picture now, see the benefits versus the risks and make decisions based on careful consideration. Right now, having Dallas on her side was a lot more important than keeping him out of her business.

"You should probably have my contact information, too," Dallas said, handing Carly a card.

She met his eyes, could see the questions there.

He knew she was struggling, knew she wanted to

say something. Maybe even knew she wanted to take back control.

She kept her mouth shut and tucked the card into her pocket. Then waited impatiently while Sergeant Wright tucked hers into a pocket in her coveralls.

"Thanks," she said, offering a quick hard smile. "I'll give you a call as soon as I arrive. I haven't gotten an update on Ms. Rothschild, but if she's awake and lucid, I'll speak with her, too. Kill three birds with one stone. So to speak."

"Killing birds with stones wouldn't be very nice, Sergeant Bliss Wright," Zane said somberly, and she smiled again. This time it was genuine and amused. Zane did that to people: made them relax and enjoy, see the fun in life rather than the trouble.

Please, God, keep him safe, Carly prayed silently. The same prayer she'd said over and over again. Not just recently. Always. From the day Zane was born.

"It's a figure of speech, hon. It just means that I can get three things done at the same time."

"Oh. That's okay, then." He glanced past her, his forehead wrinkled in the way it usually was when something was bothering him. "What are they doing over there?"

"Taking pictures."

"Is that blood on the floor?" he asked.

"It could be. We won't know for sure until the evidence lab tests it," the sergeant answered honestly, and Zane sighed.

"Well, he deserved it, I guess."

"Who?"

"The bad guy. You should never go in someone's house without permission."

"You're right about that," the sergeant said solemnly, her gaze much sharper than her voice had been. "How did he get inside?"

"He was hiding near the fence, and then we opened the back door. He had a gun, and he said I needed to come with him, but Jazz said I would come over her dead body." He frowned. "She isn't dead, is she, Mom?"

"Of course not," Carly said, hoping it was true. Praying it was true. She hadn't heard from Boone, and she was worried about what that might mean. Had something terrible happened? Was he waiting to break the news to her when they arrived?

"We need to go make sure," Zane said, darting toward the side door that opened from the kitchen. She grabbed him before he could run outside, pulling him back against her as Dallas stepped in front of them.

"Wait until I tell you to come," he said simply, and then he stepped outside into the cold gray morning and disappeared.

Carly waited, because he was the help she'd been praying and planning for. She shouldn't be intimidated by his take-charge attitude. She shouldn't be put off by it, either. She'd approached him because she was desperate. She was still desperate. Maybe more so now that Jazz had been injured and Zane nearly kidnapped.

She needed help.

He was there.

He was also different than she'd expected. More grounded and down-to-earth. The kind of guy who said what he meant and was probably honest to a fault.

The exact opposite of his brother.

Not that that mattered.

All that mattered was keeping the people she loved safe.

Dallas didn't expect there to be trouble. Not right now, anyway.

The side yard was still filled with emergency personnel, the front yard teeming with fire crew, EMTs and police officers. He spotted Chance standing near the street talking to a firefighter. A few neighbors were outside, several of them being questioned by the police. It was possible one of them had seen something, but this was a quiet neighborhood, it was early Saturday morning and the likelihood that anyone had been awake and looking out the window was slim to none. He scanned the crowd, looking for the straggler, the standout, the person who didn't belong.

Everyone seemed occupied. No gawkers standing on the sidewalk. No occupied cars sitting near the curb. Nothing to set off any alarm bells, which was good and expected.

A black Mercedes pulled up to the curb a few hundred yards away, the driver's door swinging open. A man stepped out. He was dressed in a suit, wearing a tie, his hair cut in one of those fashionable styles. He seemed to be looking at Carly's brownstone, his dark sunglasses hiding his eyes, his face turned in that direction. After a moment, he started walking toward the scene, his shoulders relaxed, everything about him reeking of confidence.

Whoever he was, he knew where he was heading. There was no hesitation. No caution. He was three houses away when he seemed to realize he was being watched. He stopped cold, pushed his glasses up on his head and eyed Dallas dispassionately.

"What's going on here?" he asked, his eyes a cold, hard gray, his brows too well shaped and perfect. *Polished*— that was the word Dallas would apply to him.

"A fire," he responded.

"At the last brownstone? My fiancée lives there." He gestured to Carly's place, a slight frown creasing his unlined forehead.

"Carly?" Dallas asked, surprised that she hadn't mentioned a significant other. She certainly hadn't acted like she had anyone to turn to. Then again, the guy in the business suit didn't look like he was capable of much more than a rousing game of golf and a few harsh words. He'd be murder in a boardroom and useless in a street fight.

"Carly? Of course not! She has a son!" he said as if that explained things.

"And?"

"I want to raise my own children. Not someone else's."

"If you adopted him, he'd be your own," Dallas pointed out, biting back harsher words. He didn't know who this guy was, but he didn't much like him. Not liking people tended to get him into trouble, because he had a big mouth and a blunt nature.

"Obviously, we have different opinions on the subject. Which doesn't matter. Carly and I are nothing to each other. I'm Brett Williams. Jasmine Rothschild is my fiancée. She lives here with Carly. Have you seen her? Is she okay?"

Dallas didn't know anything about Jazz, but after catching a glimpse of her room, he couldn't picture her with a guy who had his brows—Dallas glanced at Brett's hands—and his nails done.

Her room screamed imagination, humor, fun. This guy screamed stuck-up snob. But if he was her fiancé, he was probably worried sick and deserved whatever information Dallas could provide.

"There was some trouble at the house. Jazz was transported to the hospital with a head injury," he said.

"What? Did she fall? I've told her a dozen times not to stand on chairs to change light bulbs or grab dishes from the high cabinets. Is that what happened? Was she doing something stupid when she fell?"

"She was protecting Carly's son," Dallas replied, annoyed by the guy and his use of the word *stupid*. "If that's your idea of stupid—"

"Of course it isn't. That was a poor word choice on my part. Jazz doesn't do stupid things. She just doesn't always think things through." He sighed, running a hand over already perfectly smoothed hair. "This couldn't have happened at a worse time. We're planning a wedding. There's no time for a hospital stay."

"I'm sure she didn't allow herself to be knocked unconscious to inconvenience you," Dallas responded, still annoyed by the guy's word choices.

Brett frowned. "I'm sorry. That sounded terrible."

"Yeah. It did."

"How is she?"

"We don't know yet."

"Does Carly? Those two are as tight as thieves."

"No."

"What hospital?"

Dallas gave him the information and watched as he walked back to his car, cell phone pressed to his ear.

"Who's that?" Chance asked, jogging toward Dallas.

"Brett Williams. Jazz's fiancé."

"It didn't look like the two of you were having a pleasant conversation."

"He was upset that she was injured when they're in the middle of planning a wedding."

"Nice guy."

"I was thinking the same."

"I guess he's on the way to the hospital?" Chance nodded toward the Mercedes, watching as Brett climbed in. "I'm surprised he came here at all. Boone was supposed to call him. Carly made sure he had Jazz's phone with the contact information."

"Either Boone didn't have a chance, or he wasn't able to reach the guy. Either way, Brett ended up here."

"And you don't like him?"

"I don't know him enough to form an opinion one way or another."

"Then why did you look like you wanted to take his head off?"

Because, he could remember how he'd felt when he'd been told about Lila and the twins. He could remember the devastation and heartbreak, and he couldn't imagine anyone who really loved another person not feeling the same. He couldn't say that, so he shrugged, walking back toward the house, Chance falling into step beside him.

"You're not planning to answer the question?" he asked as they reached the side door.

"I don't have an answer. Except that I would rather see a man cry because the person he loves is hurt than hear him complain that he's being inconvenienced by the injury."

The side door was cracked open, and he touched the old wood. It swung inward.

Carly was just beyond the threshold, her hand resting on Zane's shoulder. Exhausted mother dressed in running gear. Excited kid dressed like a superhero. Something about them standing there together made Dallas's heart ache. For what they had and for what he'd lost.

He'd have turned away, but she was watching him, her eyes the soft pure green of a summer growth.

"Is everything okay?" she asked, and he nodded, afraid his voice would be gruff and rough with emotion.

"You look upset," she continued, guiding Zane closer to the door.

"Just wondering what Jazz sees in Brett."

"Did you meet him?"

"Yes."

"Then I'm not surprised you're wondering. I figure she probably sees the same thing I saw in…" Her voice trailed off and she glanced at Zane.

She didn't have to finish.

Dallas was pretty certain he knew the end: *the same thing I saw in Josh.*

If she said it, he'd have asked what that was. She lived in an area most people couldn't afford, in a beautiful home that anyone would be proud to own. She'd obviously made a good life for herself and her son. Which meant she had to be hardworking, driven and determined.

So…

Yeah.

What had someone like that seen in someone like Josh? How had a woman who knew how to work ended up with a guy who'd have done just about anything to avoid it? How had someone who was willing to fight for the people she loved ended up with a man who'd only ever fought for himself and his addiction?

He didn't ask, because Zane was there.

But he wanted to know.

He was curious about Carly, and he wasn't sure that was a good thing. Curiosity could get a man into trouble. Especially when that curiosity was focused on a woman who had summer-green eyes and a will of steel. She'd wanted help for her son, and she'd gone after it. She'd risked everything to find someone who could protect her child.

He admired that.

He admired the way she stood with her hand on her son's shoulder, her gaze on Dallas—direct and unwavering.

Admiration and curiosity, and Christmas looming on the horizon, all the old memories and heartache looming with it. If he let himself, he might get in deeper than he wanted. He might find himself getting caught up in Carly's troubles and in her life.

He wasn't sure how he felt about that, but he wasn't going to walk away. That wasn't the way his father had raised him. Timothy Morgan. The man who'd been willing to take a chance on two scrawny kids who'd been in foster care for so many years, they'd forgotten what family meant.

Did Carly know that Zane's middle name was the same as his grandfather's? Had Josh had something to do with that?

More questions that he wasn't going to ask.

"Ready?" he said instead, holding out his hand.

To his surprise, she nodded, her fingers weaving through his as she followed him outside.

SIX

Jazz looked terrible.

That was Carly's first thought. It was also her second, third and fourth.

She brushed a strand of silky blond hair from Jazz's pale cheek, trying not to notice how cool her skin felt. With an IV attached to her hand, monitors attached to her chest and a blood-pressure cuff attached to her arm, she looked frail and impossibly young. She had a bruise on her cheek that Carly hadn't noticed at the house. Scratches on her neck. Someone had put plastic bags over her fingers, and Carly assumed they planned to collect DNA evidence from under her nails. She'd saved Zane's life and risked her own, and now she was lying in a bed in the ICU, her fiancé sitting on one side of her, Carly on the other. She didn't know they were there. At least, that was what the nurse who'd been in to check her vitals had said.

Maybe she was right. Maybe not. It didn't matter. Carly had been talking to her, whispering that Zane was okay, that Jazz had saved his life, that as soon as she was better, they'd go pick out the shoes Jazz would wear with her wedding gown.

Jazz hadn't responded, but it had been enough for Carly to offer the words, to talk to her best friend the way she did every morning. They'd known each other for over a decade. They'd been housemates for six years. They were as close as sisters. Maybe closer, because there was no sibling rivalry, no jealousy.

"You're going to be okay, Jazz," Carly whispered, and Brett sighed.

"She can't hear you, Carly."

"We don't know that."

"It's what the nurse told us. Are you saying that *she* doesn't know?" He raised a raven-black eyebrow, his handsome face free from stubble, blemishes or scars. He was about as polished looking as anyone could be, and for some reason, that had always rubbed Carly the wrong way.

"I'm saying it doesn't matter."

"It should, because I'm trying to pray for her, and every time you open your mouth, I get distracted," he said, his tone clipped, his hand resting on Jazz's.

"I guess I should say I'm sorry, but I'm not. Jazz is in there somewhere, and even if her brain isn't processing what I'm saying, her neurons and synapses are," she responded, and he frowned.

"I'm the one who's sorry, Carly. I was being rude. The worry is getting to me. And the long night. I had a meeting with a client that lasted until midnight and had to take the 2:00 a.m. train into DC. I didn't get to my apartment until seven, and Jazz and I have a ten o'clock meeting with the wedding planner, so I didn't get much sleep." He patted Jazz's hand, then absently touched the huge diamond he'd presented her with when he'd proposed. "I guess I'll need to cancel that."

"I don't think Jazz is going to be able to make it, but if you think you should go, feel free." *Please.*

"Well, we *will* have to pay a cancellation fee. This late in the game, that's understood." He glanced at his watch. "And Jazz was really worried about the place settings for the reception. They're a little too plain for the event. She wanted the royal blue and ivory table-cloths, but we agreed that black and white was more formal. Now she thinks it's too spare, and she wants to switch to royal."

"I'm sure she'd be happy for you to take care of that," Carly murmured, hoping and praying that he would leave. She could see Zane outside the room, his head bobbing up and then down as he tried to get a look inside. Most of the top half of the wall was a giant window, but the lower portion was drywall. The line between the two hit right at Zane's head level. He'd been out there for twenty minutes, waiting patiently for his turn, walking from one end of the wall to the other, Dallas right beside him. Tall, handsome, stubble on his chin, his hair hanging across his forehead. Handsome. Very, very handsome. He smiled. Just a hint of a curve to his lips, and she realized she'd been staring.

She looked away, focusing her attention on Jazz. If anyone could pull her back into the world, Zane could. Carly had tried hinting to Brett that she'd like to bring Zane in, but he'd chosen to be obtuse, ignoring both the subtle hints and the not-so-subtle ones.

The rule was only two visitors at a time in the ICU. Carly would have to leave for Zane to enter, and she didn't think it was a good idea for him to be in the hospital room with Brett. The New York copyright lawyer had a lot of good qualities. Patience with kids wasn't one of them.

Zane jumped a little higher, waving wildly to get her attention.

She waved back, and Brett frowned again. "Do you think the hospital is the best place for him?"

"Where else would he be?"

"At home?"

"It's a crime scene. Even if it wasn't, I don't have anyone to watch him."

"Then who's standing out there with him? He was at your place earlier. I thought he might be a new friend."

"Dallas is my husband's brother," she corrected.

"I didn't realize you had family."

"We only met recently." She didn't explain how recently. She and Brett weren't close. They knew each other because of Jazz, but if not for her, they would have steered clear of each other at any social function. It wasn't that they disliked each other. That was much too strong a description for what Carly felt. It was more that they had nothing in common.

Except for Jazz.

"I see," Brett murmured. He patted Jazz's hand again, ran his finger lightly across the bruise on her cheek.

"She's still lovely," he commented. "Makeup should cover this, if it hasn't faded by our wedding day."

"Yes. I'm sure Jazz will be worried about that. When she wakes up," she said, unable to keep the sarcasm from her voice.

He frowned. "Every woman worries about the way she looks on the day she gets married," he replied, touching the diamond again.

She really, really wanted him to leave, because he was getting on her last nerve and pushing her to the kind of anger she didn't often feel. He'd mentioned his late night, his lack of sleep, his concern for losing money to the wedding planner. He seemed worried about a bruise that might not disappear before the wedding.

What he hadn't mentioned, what he didn't seem all that concerned about, was Jazz's condition. The nurse had given them almost no information. She'd said the CAT scan results were pending and that Jazz was stable. For now. Brett hadn't asked questions, hadn't requested a meeting with the doctor. He might be Jazz's choice for a lifelong partner, but he wasn't even close to good enough for her.

The words were on the tip of Carly's tongue, and she was just irritated enough to say them, but someone rapped on the window. She glanced over, saw that Dallas had lifted Zane onto his shoulders. Zane was tapping on the glass, grinning from ear to ear. There was nothing unusual about his smile or his face, but the image of the two caught her attention and held it. The line of Zane's jaw, the angle of his chin and the shape of his eyes were so like Dallas's, her breath caught. It made sense. They were related. But they could have been father and son. That was what struck her—the obvious genetic link between the two, the family resemblance.

The bond that seemed to already be forming.

She wasn't sure what she would do with that.

She'd never deny her son the opportunity to know his paternal family. Not if they wanted to know him. But Dallas...

He might be a problem.

She met his eyes, and he smiled again. This time a

full-out grin that made her heart jump. She didn't want a man in her life. She'd made that decision a long time ago. But she'd invited Dallas. She'd nearly begged him to help her. Now he was out in the hall with her son, smiling in a way that made her heart want to melt. He gestured for her to come out of the room, and she stood, moving toward him without thinking about all the reasons why she shouldn't.

"Are you leaving?" Brett asked, patting Jazz's hand one more time and then standing.

"Just stepping into the hall for a minute. Zane has been waiting for a while, and he's probably getting restless."

Brett glanced at the window and offered one of the smiles he reserved for elderly people and kids. Broad, toothy and fake. "I'm being selfish," he said. "He deserves to have some time with his aunt."

"You have every right to stay as long as you want," she responded, because if Jazz could hear, it was what she'd want Carly to say.

"That goes without saying, Carly, but that doesn't mean I should steal time from a little boy who's probably very scared by everything he's seeing at the hospital."

Zane didn't look scared, but Carly went with it. "Hospitals can be intimidating for kids."

"Exactly. So I'll disappear for a little bit. Maybe an hour? That should give Zane plenty of time."

"An hour is more than enough time."

"I might be a little longer. If I'm going to leave her, I may as well do something productive for my future wife."

"You're going to meet with the wedding planner?" she guessed.

"And get a bite to eat. I haven't had anything since my dinner appointment yesterday." He leaned down and kissed Jazz's cheek, but he didn't say goodbye to her. Obviously, he thought that would be a waste of time. "If things change, give me a ring. I won't be more than twenty minutes away."

"I will."

"Thanks, Carly. You're a good friend. Jazz and I really appreciate that about you."

He walked into the hall, offering Zane a quick high five as he moved past.

Carly was right behind him.

She reached for Zane, tugging him down.

As she set Zane on his feet, Dallas turned, and suddenly they were face-to-face, his ocean-blue eyes staring into hers.

"You look unhappy," he said quietly.

"I'm worried."

"About Jazz?"

"Yes."

"And about me and Zane?" he continued, and she couldn't deny it.

"Just about you," she blurted out, and he chuckled.

"At least you're honest."

"I've been lied to a lot in my life. I try not to do it to other people."

"I live by the same philosophy, so don't worry too much."

"Can I go in, Mom?" Zane interrupted, walking to the threshold of the room and peering inside.

It was the perfect distraction, and she went with it, hurrying to his side. "Only with me. They don't let kids go in without adults."

"Is she sleeping?" he whispered.

"Sort of." She led him into the room, studiously avoiding looking in Dallas's direction. Which, of course, meant that she really wanted to look. She liked his smile, his easy way with Zane. More than anything, she liked the fact that he was there, standing outside the room, playing bodyguard to a child he barely knew.

Her phone buzzed as Zane took a seat next to Jazz and lifted her limp hand, the plastic bag rustling. "She has bags on her hands," he commented.

"They do that sometimes."

"Yeah, because she punched the guy right in the face, and maybe she got blood and stuff under her nails."

"You've been watching too many of those crime shows, buddy."

"I think I watched just enough." He leaned across the crisp white sheet and studied Jazz's face.

"You're very brave, Aunt Jazzy," he whispered, his expression more somber than Carly had ever seen it. "And I love you very much. Also, I have a secret." He leaned even closer, whispering about his new uncle who was probably a superhero, because he was taller than anyone Zane had ever seen.

Carly listened with half an ear as she pulled out her phone and scanned the message from her boss, Michael Raintree. He lived in her neighborhood and had seen the commotion at her house. He wanted to make sure she was okay. She typed a quick response and then checked her emails. She had a few offers for freelance work restoring old family heirlooms. Based on the queries she'd had in the months since she'd moved to DC, she wasn't going to have to worry about finding work if the Smithsonian didn't offer her a salaried position when her contract was up.

Michael had assured her that they would. As the director of operations, he had the most say when it came to hiring. He'd been the one to put Carly's name in for the contracted job. He'd also encouraged her to take it. They'd been friends since college. They'd both apprenticed with a master gemstone cutter whose expertise was in antique cuts and tools.

Carly had excelled. Michael had struggled. He'd never seemed to care, though. He'd encouraged her, cheered her on, kept in touch with her when she'd married Josh, offered her advice when she was widowed. By that time, he'd been married, his wife pregnant with their first child. He'd established himself in the New York museum scene and was head curator at the American Museum of Natural History. A year later, he took a job at the Smithsonian in DC.

He was, in Carly's opinion, an all-around good guy.

If he said she'd be offered a salaried position, she probably would be, but she didn't believe in taking chances. She'd already accepted a few small jobs, and she planned to meet with another potential client Monday afternoon. She could make excellent money working freelance, and there were plenty of museums in the area that might have contract work for her to do.

Not that any of that would matter if Jazz didn't improve.

Another email came through, and she opened it, her heart stopping as she saw the contents: a photo of Zane sitting on Dallas's shoulders and the message *Say one word about the gems, and he dies.*

She looked up, expecting to see someone at the window staring at her.

Dallas was there. Boone had joined him. They were sipping coffee and discussing something. She stood, moving closer to the window and looking out into the corridor. There were a few nurses, a janitor, a man pushing a cart filled with food trays.

Someone tapped the glass, and she jumped, her gaze darting in the direction of the sound. Dallas was there, Boone just a few inches away. They were both watching her.

She knew how she must look—wild-eyed and scared—but she didn't care. Someone had sent her a photo of her son. One that had been taken moments ago.

Whoever it was had to be close.

"Stay right there, buddy," she said to Zane. "I'm just going out in the hall for a second."

"But you said kids couldn't be in the room without an adult."

"I'll send an adult in." She walked across the room, her legs stiff with anxiety. One wrong move and her entire world would fall apart. She felt it like she felt her heart beating in her ears.

"But, Mom—"

"Stay here." She stepped out into the hall.

Dallas's expression had changed.

He knew something was wrong, but he was acting like everything was just right, moving toward her, sliding his hands around her waist and tugging her into his arms.

She fit there perfectly.

The thought flitted through her head, but she didn't have time to dwell on it.

He was leaning toward her, his lips brushing her forehead. To anyone watching, they'd look like a couple exchanging a comforting embrace.

"What's wrong?" he murmured, so quietly she almost didn't hear.

"Someone emailed a photo of Zane sitting on your shoulders," she replied just as quietly.

His hands tightened on her waist. Other than that, nothing changed. Not his expression, his posture, his tone.

"Okay," he said, brushing a strand of hair from her cheek, his fingers lingering. She could feel the warmth of them spreading through her, chasing away the fear and dread.

"It isn't," she responded, her voice shaking as much from his touch as from her terror.

"It will be." His lips brushed her cheek this time. "Go back in the room and text me the photo." He pulled her in for another hug. For show, she knew, but it felt better than anything had in a very long time.

"She'll be okay," he continued loudly enough for anyone nearby to hear.

She nodded, because she couldn't speak. Her throat was clogged with emotion. Only half of it terror.

He stepped back, his hands dropping away, and she was cold again. Freezing. All the fear rushing back.

She shoved it down and hurried back into the room, taking a seat next to Jazz's bed and doing exactly what Dallas had asked.

It took three seconds to read the text.

Dallas waited another few minutes before he sent it

to Boone. They didn't need to discuss it. They knew what it meant.

"You want me to go take over so you can bring your lady for some coffee?" Boone suggested idly. Not even a hint of anxiety in his voice.

"Sounds like a plan. I don't get to spend enough time alone with her," Dallas responded, playing along for whoever might be listening.

No sense in giving the perp a warning. Let him think that Carly was still going along with the plan.

Seconds later, Boone was in the room and Carly was out of it. She looked anxious, tense and terrified. Exactly what the perp expected and wanted.

"Hey, hon," he said, taking her hand, dropping a kiss on her knuckles. "How about some coffee?"

"I don't want to leave Zane and Jazz," she said, and he knew she meant it. No playing along. No putting on a show. She wasn't planning to leave.

"I think," he said, "that Jazz would expect you to."

"I—"

"Boone is with them." He wasn't going to take no for an answer. He wanted to see if he could spot the perp, but he wasn't leaving all three potential victims in one place. Separate them. Let the perp try to decide how to respond. That was the plan. "I think we could both use some new scenery. Who knows who we'll run into while we're away?"

She got it then. Finally.

"Right. You're right. Let's go."

He walked beside her, scanning the doorways on either side of the hall. It would have been simple enough for the perp to step inside a room, but they all had glass windows, making it easy for the nurses to keep an eye on the critical patients and difficult for the photographer to hide. Dallas could see family members sitting at bedsides, most of them bent over phones or leaning in toward patients, keeping silent vigil. Maybe praying.

He'd been on the other side of the glass. He'd been the one lying in the bed. He knew the heavy weight of fear and anxiety the waiting loved ones carried with them. He'd felt it every time he'd opened his eyes and seen his parents sitting by his bed.

He also knew that it would be impossible for a stranger to walk in without the family reacting.

Thus far, he'd seen no sign that anyone had been disturbed. No sign that a stranger had barged into a patient's room.

He tried a storage door to his left. It was locked. Up ahead, double doors led out of the ICU. A desk sat nearby, several nurses eyeing monitors there. Everyone seemed to be going about their morning as usual, but someone who didn't belong had been here.

"Do you think he's already gone?" Carly asked, her voice whisper soft.

"Leaving would have been the smart thing to do, but he stood a dozen feet away and snapped a photo of me and Zane, so he's probably not all that smart."

"You're assuming he's a man."

"I'm not assuming anything except that he's probably not the guy I shot in front of my house." He hadn't spoken to the police about that, but he'd have to. Soon. There'd been blood left at Carly's house and blood in the street at his place. Plenty of DNA to run through the system. If they got a name, Dallas could use HEART resources to find the suspect. He wasn't sure the police would approve, and he was equally unsure whether or not he cared.

He pulled out his phone, magnifying the photo so he could see the details more clearly.

"What are you looking for?" she asked, leaning in, her arm pressed against his. He caught a whiff of coffee and soap, flowers and sunshine. She'd felt good in his arms. Like she belonged there. If he'd known that would be the case, he'd never have hugged her, never have let his lips trail across her forehead and cheek. She was a habit he could easily form, an addiction he wouldn't mind having.

He frowned, forcing himself to focus on the photo and on the conversation. "I'm trying to figure out exactly where he was standing. There was a good reflection on the glass. I could see people moving to either side of the hall. I think I'd have noticed if someone was shooting pictures with his phone."

"He held the phone low and angled it up." She pointed to the screen, her short nails unvarnished, the tiny white scars on her knuckles showing clearly in the fluorescent light. "He probably wasn't even looking through the lens. He was probably taking random shots, hoping to get a decent one. He didn't even need a good one. He just needed one that would prove he'd been here and was close."

"Right." At least a dozen people had walked through the hall while Zane had been on his shoulders. Half of them were probably visitors. Most would've been holding cell phones. He'd let the DC police know, and they could pull the security footage, but that didn't satisfy Dallas. He wanted the guy caught now. Not three or four days or weeks or months from now.

The double doors opened, and two nurses walked through. A man followed behind—dressed in scrubs, a stethoscope hanging haphazardly around his neck. A doctor or nurse, but Dallas couldn't see a name tag or badge. His hair was plastered to his head, a pair of glasses perched on his nose, and he looked like any other doctor or nurse walking through the corridor— serious expression, rubber-soled shoes, one hand in the pocket of his scrubs. He moved with quick, purposeful strides, and Dallas wouldn't have thought much about him except that his gaze was fixed on the floor. Studiously and purposely avoiding eye contact.

That was a red flag that Dallas wouldn't ignore.

He waited until the guy passed, let him round the corner and then followed, Carly hurrying along beside him.

She didn't ask where they were going. He assumed she already knew. She'd been watching the guy, too, her smooth brow furrowed, her eyes narrowed. Instinct was everything in Dallas's business, and he thought his instinct and Carly's were the same right now. The guy was hiding something.

It was possible he was the on-call doctor, trying to avoid patients' families so he didn't have to deal with their questions, their tears, their heartache. That would make sense. It would fit the situation. It would be the best-case scenario.

The problem was, Dallas rarely dealt with best-case. Usually he walked into the worst thing he'd imagined.

He and Carly rounded the corner. Jazz's room was in the middle of the hall, not far from the nurses' station. The guy they were following scanned room numbers, knocked on Jazz's door and stepped inside. Dallas moved forward, walking past the windows and looking inside.

Boone was standing, positioned between himself and Zane, but the doctor or nurse or whoever he was seemed to have no interest in either of them. He was leaning over Jazz, listening to her heart, checking her temperature, adjusting the IV line and doing all the normal things a nurse did.

There appeared to be no reason to be alarmed, but worry nudged at the back of Dallas's mind, anxiety swirling in his gut. The nurse took a syringe from his pocket, squirted fluid in the air as if checking to be sure there were no air bubbles. Odd, but not improbable— except that the syringe hadn't been capped. It had come out of his pocket ready to use.

Boone said something, and the guy shrugged, reaching for the IV line.

Boone grabbed his arm, pulling him away, and Dallas shoved open the door, the muted sound of Christmas music following him as he grabbed the guy by the back of the shirt and dragged him away. The man in scrubs cursed, grabbing the IV pole, yanking it onto its side, crushing the bag of fluid and the lines under his feet as he dropped the needle and pulled a knife from beneath his shirt.

An alarm sounded, the quick sharp chirp filling the room.

Boone and Zane were gone, probably hiding behind the locked bathroom door. That was protocol, protection of innocent life always the team's priority. Carly stood near the door, scanning the room, probably looking for a weapon she could use to help. And Dallas was eye to eye with a guy who'd probably do anything to get away before the police showed up.

"I just want to leave," he said reasonably. "You let me do that, and no one will get hurt."

"No one is going to get hurt if you put the knife down," Dallas countered.

"Sorry. Not going to happen." He slashed the air, the blade rasping through the empty space between them.

Dallas had a gun, but he didn't pull it. He wouldn't fire it in the hospital and risk the bullet going through a wall or window and hurting an innocent bystander.

Carly stepped farther into the room, moving into Dallas's periphery.

"Don't," Dallas cautioned. The last thing he wanted was her getting in between him and the knife.

Carly froze, stopping short a few feet away.

The perp scowled.

"Back off, buddy," the guy said, the knife still pointed in Dallas's direction. His hand was fisted around it, his knuckles white from the strength of his grip.

He was afraid, and scared people did stupid things. Like lose their focus, forget what they should be concentrating on.

"Put the knife down," Dallas countered.

"I don't take orders from anyone."

"So you're the boss, huh? The one who called the shots and decided to attack an incapacitated woman?"

"I wasn't attacking anyone," he responded, falling for Dallas's bait, chasing the verbal rabbit, the knife lowering a little.

"What do you call trying to kill someone?"

"I wasn't trying to kill her!" he nearly shouted.

"You were putting something in her IV. What was it?"

"Just something to make her heart rate increase. He wanted a distraction, but he didn't say anything about murder." The blade of the knife was pointing toward the floor, the man's dark eyes narrowed, his skin ruddy with emotion.

"Who is *he*?"

"I don't know, and I don't care. If he's good for the money, it doesn't matter." His attention shifted to Carly.

She was standing directly in the path of the only exit.

"Move!" the perp barked, forgetting, it seemed, that Dallas was a much bigger threat.

Because scared people really did make a lot of mistakes.

Dallas dived toward him, knocking the knife from his hand and tackling him to the ground.

SEVEN

Dallas had the guy pinned in seconds, forearm thrust under his chin, arm pressed against his trachea. He'd gone from defensive posture to dangerous in three seconds flat. Carly took a step back, edging toward the door.

But of course, she couldn't leave.

She had to make sure Jazz was okay; she had to check on Zane.

She changed trajectory, edging by the two men and lifting the IV pole as Dallas barked, "Who's paying you?"

"I don't know," the guy gasped.

"I think you're lying." Dallas's voice was ice-cold, his expression hard. He didn't look like the uncle who'd lifted Zane to his shoulders or the guy who'd smiled at him because Zane was the kind of kid everyone smiled at. He didn't look like the man who'd pulled Carly into his arms, kissed her forehead, her cheek. Stilled her fears for long enough to get her thinking again.

He didn't look like any of those things.

He looked like the person described in the news stories Josh had collected—tough, driven, hard. The

kind of person who got things done, who didn't let anyone stand in the way of his mission.

"I'm not lying. My buddy set me up with the gig."

"You call killing a woman a gig?" Dallas didn't move, but Carly had the distinct impression he could have easily crushed the guy's windpipe. A little more pressure, a little more effort, and the knife-wielding man would die.

"Dallas," she began, planning to warn him, to encourage him to back away from the fight.

"I told you, I wasn't trying to kill her. I was just creating a distraction, so…" His voice trailed off.

"So what?"

"I have a kid, man!" he responded. "He's sick, and I don't have insurance. I need the money."

"I think that's a lie, too," Dallas retorted, his face just as hard, his tone just as cold. "So how about you try again?"

"It's not a lie. He's two floors up in the children's cancer unit. Loyal Richards. You can check it out."

"The police can, but it won't matter. It's sure not going to make anyone more friendly with you, and it isn't going to keep you from going to jail."

"My kid is sick," the man said again, and for the first time, he looked afraid. "I can't go to jail."

"You should have thought of that before you came in here."

"I needed the money."

"There are other ways of getting money. Ways that don't involve hurting other people."

"My son—"

"Your son wants a father he can look up to." Dallas

yanked him to his feet as a security guard barreled into the room.

The rest happened quickly. Another security officer arrived. A nurse sidled into the room, the DC police right behind her. There were lots of voices, noise and activity, and Jazz was still and silent on the bed. Her face pale, her eyes closed. Not even a flicker of movement.

Carly touched her cheek. "Hey, you in there?"

She didn't get a response, but she thought Jazz's eyelids fluttered.

"Everything is going to be okay," Carly continued, hoping she was right, that Jazz would get better, that she'd have her New Year's Eve wedding, that her life would be the wonderful romantic dream she'd told Carly she wanted when they were college students sharing a dorm.

Things had been so much less complicated then. Jazz had been the dreamer. Carly had been the practical one. They'd liked each other enough to room together for two years. Then life had happened. Carly had met Josh, and she'd fallen hard, and everything that had been easy became complicated.

"I need to get in there, hon," a nurse said, nudging her out of the way.

Two other nurses converged on the bed, and Carly was displaced, standing in the middle of a dozen people but suddenly completely alone. This was one of those times when it would feel good to know that she had a husband or sister, mother or father or brother she could call, someone who cared enough, was invested enough in her life to leave whatever he or she was doing and rush to her side.

"You okay?" Dallas said, and she realized that he

was standing beside her, studying her face, looking for an answer. All the hardness was gone, the coldness replaced by warm concern. He was a different man from the one who'd had his forearm to a guy's throat, and she couldn't help wondering which man was the real one.

She wanted to believe this one was—the one who seemed to care, whose palm slid up her arm, cupped her nape, kneaded the tense muscles there.

She could have melted into a puddle on the floor.

She could have leaned toward him, allowed herself to dwell in the comfort of the moment.

She stepped away instead.

"I need to check on Zane." She turned away.

She'd made her mistake. She'd done her time.

She had Zane because of that, and she wouldn't regret it, but she wouldn't repeat it, either. And the first step to repeating it was being interested, asking questions, trying to get to know the person behind the handsome face and the stunning eyes.

It all led to a broken heart.

That was how it had played out with Josh. Based on her track record with men, that shouldn't have been surprising. She'd dated a lot in high school. She'd been with guys who'd used her and tossed her aside. Then her perspective had changed during her senior year; her values had shifted. She'd realized she was going down the same path her mother had, and she'd been determined to change. So she'd shaped up. She'd given up the dead-end relationships, the useless flirtations. She'd always been a good student, but she'd become an exceptional one.

College had been her goal, and she'd achieved it.

She'd thought she'd achieve all the other things, too. The husband and kids and happy life together.

She scowled, raising her hand to knock on the bathroom door.

"You can knock, but Boone isn't going to answer," Dallas said, and she swung around, found herself looking straight into his eyes.

"I want to see my son."

"Do you want your son to see this?" He gestured toward the bed, where nurses were working to set up a new IV. Then to the security guards and police who'd surrounded the attacker. The knife was still on the floor, the syringe a few feet away.

Of course she didn't want Zane to see any of it.

"Boone can let me in. Zane doesn't have to see anything."

"Except you looking terrified?"

He had a point, even if she didn't want to admit it. When it came to Zane, she'd always been the decision maker. There'd never been a second parent to consult with, no grandparents. Jazz mostly kept her nose out of decisions regarding Zane. She didn't give unsolicited advice or tell Carly what she should or should not be doing with her son.

So having someone telling her what was best for Zane was new, and she didn't particularly like it.

She was pretty sure Dallas understood that.

"You want me to butt out," he said, as if he'd read her mind.

It wasn't a question, but she answered anyway. "I'm not going to deny that."

"And I'm not going to remind you that you approached me and asked for my help."

"You just did," she pointed out, and he smiled.

She couldn't help herself. She smiled, too.

"That's better," he said, his expression gentle and open. She could have fallen into it if she'd let herself. What she couldn't do was look away. She couldn't stop studying the lines and angles of his face, the ocean-blue depths of his eyes.

"Ms. Kelley?" someone called, and she used that as the perfect excuse to break eye contact.

Sergeant Wright was walking into the room, her expression stern, her dark eyes scanning the crowd before settling on Carly. "The hospital has graciously allowed us the use of a conference room. We'll all be more comfortable there. One of my officers will escort you, and I'll join you once things are settled here."

"I'd rather wait for Zane."

"It will be easier for everyone if you don't," she responded, waving an officer over.

"Easier how?"

"We don't need this many people in the room. Besides, the sooner your interview begins, the sooner it will be over and we can move on to Zane. I'm sure you'd like to get out of here at some point today."

"I would, but I don't want to leave my son down here alone."

"He's not alone. There are a half dozen law enforcement officers in this room. Plus your friend," the sergeant pointed out. "And none of us are going to let anything happen to Zane."

"Boone and I will make sure he's okay," Dallas assured her, his hand cupping her elbow as he walked her to the door.

She could feel the warmth of his fingers through

her coat, and she told herself that it didn't feel nice, that she hadn't missed the sweetness of someone else's touch, the comforting feeling of warm hands against chilly skin.

She hadn't realized how cold she was until he released her and stepped back into the room, leaving her in the hallway with a tall redheaded officer, a hammering heart and the bittersweet memory of all the things she'd once thought she'd have.

A two-hour interrogation by the DC police was not the way Dallas had hoped to spend his day, but that was exactly how things were playing out. He might not have been so impatient about it if he hadn't spent the previous forty minutes talking to the Montgomery County Police about the incident in front of his house. They'd asked questions and had seemed satisfied with his answers. They'd also been willing to fill him in on what they'd discovered at the scene—or rather, not discovered: a body or, aside from a few drops of blood on the pavement, evidence that anyone had been seriously injured. Dallas was confident his bullet had struck the perp, but he'd kept that information to himself. If the guy had been mortally wounded, the K-9 unit that had been dispatched would have found him. According to the officers who'd interviewed Dallas, the dogs had followed a scent trail to the same parking lot Carly had used and lost it there.

Still, they'd seemed more than willing to believe Dallas's account. They had a witness, they'd said. A neighbor who'd seen most of what had happened. His version had corroborated Dallas's, and that, it seemed, was that.

They were satisfied. Dallas was free to return home.

Except that he wasn't.

The DC police wanted some of his time, too. Actually, lots of his time.

He glanced at his watch, tapping his fingers against the faux-wood table that sat in the back of what looked like a classroom, with a whiteboard at one end, long tables lined up in rows and spindly folding chairs pushed beneath them facing the board. He wasn't sure what kind of teaching they might do at a general hospital, but he imagined they could fit a hundred students in a space this size.

Dallas eyed the officers who sat across the table from him. They were jotting notes and frowning. He'd answered dozens of questions, maybe hundreds. He'd responded with candor and honesty. He'd held nothing back, because there was nothing to hold on to. He'd been dragged into something he knew nothing about by a woman he hadn't known twenty-four hours ago.

Except that the officers who were questioning him didn't seem to buy it. Funny how the truth was often stranger than fiction.

"So, what you're saying," one of them said, pausing to lift the tablet he'd been writing on, "is that you never met Carly Kelley before this morning?"

"That's correct."

"And you're also saying that she's your sister-in-law?"

"In legal terms. Yes."

"Legal terms? Can you clarify that?"

"She was married to my brother. He died seven years ago. I didn't meet Carly when they were married."

"That seems unusual. Don't you think?"

"My brother and I were estranged." He managed to

keep impatience and irritation out of his voice. Barely. He'd answered this same question at least ten times, and—he decided, shoving away from the table and standing—he wasn't answering it again.

"Is something wrong, Mr. Morgan?" the younger of the two officers asked. She had close-cropped brown hair colored deep burgundy at the ends, her face perfectly made-up, her expression a mixture of surprise and irritation.

"Only the fact that you've asked me the same question a dozen times."

"I'm sorry if that seems like a burden. We're just trying to make sure we get your story straight." She stood.

"It couldn't get any straighter, Officer. I gave you the facts. I'm sorry you're not satisfied with them."

"It's not that we're not satisfied. It just seems odd to us that Ms. Kelley's house was set on fire right after you met."

"The fact that her house was set on fire isn't strange in and of itself?" he asked.

"Of course it is. But we like to look for patterns, find connections—"

"Beat a question into the ground and hope that doing so will give you a different answer?"

"We're trying to be thorough." She'd followed him to the door. But she couldn't keep him from leaving, and they both knew it. To her credit, she didn't even try.

"Look, Mr. Morgan," she said as he stepped into the hall, "I know it feels as if we're treating you like a criminal, but getting the facts right, making sure that when we make an arrest it's the right guy, is our highest priority."

"I don't feel like I'm being treated like a criminal.

I feel like I'm wasting my time. You have my contact information. If you come up with any new questions, give me a call." He walked away, heading for the bank of elevators at the end of the hall, his knee throbbing a loud and annoying protest.

He'd done too much. For sure.

This was what he'd spent the past few years living for—helping people, making a difference, doing what he hadn't been able to do for his wife and children.

He swallowed down the bitter taste of regret, the sour taste of guilt.

There was nothing he could have done.

He'd been told that dozens of times by dozens of well-meaning people. Even if he'd been in the driver's seat when the semitruck had crossed the center lane, he couldn't have changed the outcome. He'd lived because he was young and healthy. Lila had been seven months pregnant. The injuries that he'd survived probably would have killed her. They definitely would have killed the babies.

He knew the facts, but they didn't change anything. They didn't take away the feeling of helpless rage when he woke up from the nightmares—headlights and brakes squealing and Lila's scream.

The last sound she'd ever make.

He slammed his hand on the elevator button, stepping inside and waiting impatiently for it to carry him up to the sixth floor. Boone and Chance were sitting in on the interview with Zane. *His nephew.* The more he saw the kid, the more obvious the resemblance to Josh was. He couldn't dismiss it. Nor could he convince himself that Carly was lying. He wasn't sure why she hadn't bothered contacting his family before. Maybe she'd believed whatever lies Josh had told her—and there was no doubt he'd told her plenty. Josh had been great at pretending. He'd even had Dallas fooled for a while.

None of that mattered, though. Zane was family, and that mattered way more than decade-old hurts.

Faith first. Family second.

That was his parents' mantra. It was why they'd put up with Josh for so many years, why they'd stuck by him through two stints in rehab. Why they would have forgiven him if he'd ever apologized for stealing their money and Mom's jewelry, for breaking their trust. Again and again and again.

But he'd never apologized, because he'd never thought he was wrong. In his opinion, the world owed him for the mess he'd been born into, and he'd made sure that his adoptive parents paid the debt. He'd stolen a car, taken valuables and money, and finally disappeared for good. No note to say where he'd gone. No phone call to let them know he was okay. He'd just walked off and never returned. When they'd finally found him, he'd made it very clear he wanted nothing to do with the family. He'd obviously meant it.

Josh had never told their parents that he'd married. Dallas had been the one to let them know. Their mother had cried. He'd never given them the joy of knowing they would have a grandson, either. He'd taken everything they'd been willing to give and withheld the one thing they'd wanted—his love.

Dallas had tried to make up for it, but love unreturned was as painful as love dying.

The elevator doors opened, and Dallas stalked out, tired, frustrated, angry.

The day had taken a much darker turn than he'd

expected. And now he was thinking about things better forgotten.

He'd loved Josh once upon a time. He'd been the older brother, the protector, the one who could make things better. They'd lived in a meth house until Dallas was nine, watching adults smoke and shoot up and sniff and pass out. There'd never been enough food, enough heat, enough clothes. He'd learned to cook eggs and to steal milk. He'd figured out how to open canned soup and heat it on the stove. He'd learned to read so that he could teach his brother. He'd been the one to give baths, help with homework, tie shoes, get Josh up for school, and he'd done it all while their mother slept off her latest bender or entertained her newest guy friend.

When they'd entered foster care, it had been a respite from the stress of too much responsibility at too young an age, but that had been tough, too. Good foster parents followed by not-so-good ones. One couple made them sleep on wood pallets in the basement.

In the end, the state had placed them with the Morgans. Life had gotten much better. Dallas had taken advantage of the opportunities he'd been given. Josh had taken the path of least resistance, going in the same direction their mother had.

Drugs. Stealing. Drinking.

He'd broken their new parents' hearts so many times those first few months, Dallas had been certain the placement would be dissolved. Instead, the Morgans had adopted them, given everything they could to be the best parents they could.

Faith first. Family second. Without any expectations. Without any need for thanks.

Dallas had learned a lot from their example. He was still learning. If the twins had lived…

He shut the thought down. Shut out the past.

Dwelling there didn't lead to a good night's sleep.

The conference room was just ahead, and Boone was leaning against the wall beside the door, munching what looked like a sugar cookie. "Hungry?" he asked as Dallas approached.

"No."

"You look hungry." He held out the package of cookies. "I got these from a vending machine."

"Like I said, I'm not hungry."

"You're mad. What's got you riled up? The situation or the fact that you had no idea you had a nephew until this morning?"

"All of the above. Are they done in there?"

"No. Been asking that little boy questions for over an hour, filling him up with cookies and soda and pizza, not letting him go home. That got me riled, and I finally decided to step out and take a break before I said something Chance might regret." He finished off the cookie, brushed crumbs from his hands and popped another one in his mouth.

"You're not worried about regretting it yourself?"

Boone raised a dark red brow. "We've known each other for a long time. Have you ever known me to say something I regretted?"

"I guess I haven't."

"Exactly. I say what I mean, and I don't back down from the consequences. I've got kids, Dallas, and I keep thinking about how I'd feel if that was one of mine sitting in there, but Chance told me to keep a low profile. He doesn't want to be stonewalled by the investigating officers, and he's feeling like that could happen if we make any missteps."

"He's got a point, like always, but I think he's lost sight of the big picture. We can investigate, and we can keep Carly and her family safe. We don't need the DC police to do that for us. I'm surprised Carly is allowing things to go on this long."

"She tried to stop them forty minutes ago, thirty minutes ago, twenty minutes ago, but they're bulldozing her, reminding her over and over again that she has to cooperate if she wants to keep her son safe."

"And Chance is allowing *that*?"

"He stepped out to make a few phone calls. He doesn't want Carly and Zane to go back to their place, and he's trying to set up a safe location before he gets them out of here."

"That's nice," Dallas said, all the irritation he'd been feeling, all the anger, still simmering. Only now he had a place to direct it. "But you've known me a long time, Boone," he said, and Boone grinned.

"That's true."

"And in all the time you've known me, have you ever known me to worry about saying something Chance would regret?"

"I don't believe I have."

"And have you ever known me to worry about stepping on the toes of the local authorities?"

"Can't say I've known you to do that, either."

"Chance told you to keep a low profile. He didn't say a word to me. I'm loyal to the team, and I play by the rules. As long as the other team does the same."

"I was hoping you'd say that." Boone finished off a cookie, neatly folded the package to close it up again and put it back in his pocket. "Come on. Let's do this thing."

Dallas's thoughts exactly.

He opened the conference room door and did exactly what had to be done.

EIGHT

Three in the morning was as good a time as any to think things through, and Carly was thinking about a lot of things.

For example: when a person had been living on her own terms for most of her life, a week was a long time to live on someone else's. A week was also a long time to wait for a best friend to wake up from a coma. It was a long time to keep a son home from school.

A week, which usually flew by, was a long time when most of your life was on hold.

And hers was, because she'd agreed to move into Dallas's house, share a room with her son, let a group of people she didn't know take charge of her life. She'd asked for help, and she'd gotten it. Not just from Dallas. Several members of HEART were staying at the house and offering round-the-clock protection. They told her where she could go and when. They decided who would escort her. For Zane's sake, she'd been doing everything they asked.

Anything to keep him safe.

She sighed, pushing aside the covers and easing out of bed. The floor creaked as she walked across the room and checked on Zane. He was sleeping soundly. Just like always. It would take more than her opening the door for him to rouse, but she moved quietly anyway, shuffling across the room and putting her hand on the old glass doorknob. She stood there for a moment, listening to the old house settling, the walls sighing. If she hadn't known better, she'd have believed the house was empty.

But, of course, she did know.

Aside from Dallas, two HEART operatives were there. If they were following the pattern they had every other night, one of them was sitting in the living room watching live feed from exterior security cameras. The other was on the couch nearby, sleeping or reading or doing whatever security specialists did when they weren't watching monitors. Dallas was in his room. Straight across the hall. If she opened her door, she'd see his.

She knew that just like she knew what he looked like first thing in the morning when his eyes were still red-rimmed from sleep. She knew how he looked with a coffee mug in his hand and with his hair mussed from his evening run. She knew the sound of his voice, his laughter, his deep-throated bellow when he was playing David and Goliath with Zane.

She knew him, and she was pretty certain he knew her. They'd spent nearly every waking hour together this past week. Her personal bodyguard was what he called himself.

She called him a complication that she didn't need and a craving that she couldn't seem to ignore. Every morning, she decided that she would ask someone else to accompany her to work. Every evening, she promised herself that she'd be in her room before he came back from his run. Neither of those things ever happened. Her fault. Not his. He wasn't putting any pressure on her, wasn't demanding anything except that she follow the rules. She could have insisted that they not spend so much time together. She hadn't, because she hadn't wanted to.

She frowned, easing the door open and stepping into the hall. Dallas's door was closed, no light seeping out from under it. If she was quiet enough, she might be able to slip past without waking him. She turned toward the back of the house, heading for an old servant's staircase that led into the kitchen. Chance and Jackson Miller were on duty tonight, and she wasn't in the mood for conversation. Hopefully, she could avoid them, too.

"Going somewhere?" Dallas asked, his voice a low rumble in the dark hall.

She swung around, realized he was standing just inches away. "You're awake."

"So are you," he pointed out.

"I couldn't sleep."

"Must be an epidemic," he replied, his voice gruff and raspy.

She tried to see him through the darkness, but he was nothing but a shadowy blur. "I know why I'm awake. What's keeping you up?"

"Do you want the easy answer or the hard one?"

"Which do you want to give?" she asked, her hand moving of its own accord, settling on his shoulder. Just that touch connected them, but she felt every breath he took, felt the tension in his muscles.

"You never asked me why I sent a card instead of attending Josh's funeral," he responded.

"You were estranged."

"Not enough to keep me from attending."

"Okay. I'll bite. Why weren't you there?"

"I was in the hospital recovering from the accident that killed my wife. She was seven months pregnant with twins that were due on Christmas Eve. They were killed, too."

"Dallas—" She had no idea what she planned to say. She couldn't think of one word that would make any kind of difference.

"You're sorry? Yeah. I've heard that a thousand times before," he said, lifting her hand from his shoulder with a gentleness that made her heart ache. "I appreciate the sympathy, but it can't bring them back."

"And it can't make this time of year any easier."

"That, either." He squeezed her hand and released it, turning away.

She thought he was going to his room. She also thought that she should let him. Putting a door between them was a good idea. A couple of doors was even better, but she couldn't let him go. Not when she'd heard the weariness in his voice. Not when she knew the truth about why he was awake.

"I was going down to the kitchen." She spoke into the silence, the words hanging lamely in the air.

For a moment, she thought he wouldn't respond.

"I'm glad to hear you weren't trying to leave the house," he finally said.

"I've been here a week. I haven't done it yet."

"You've been here a week," he agreed. "And you're getting restless." Not a question, but she nodded, knowing he probably couldn't see her through the darkness.

"I'm used to running every day." She was also used to making her own decisions and doing her own things.

"I'd take you when I go tomorrow, but it would be too dangerous." He'd turned toward her again. She could see the outline of his shoulders, his head, his long legs.

"It's already tomorrow," she pointed out, her pulse jumping as he walked toward her.

She wasn't a kid.

She knew how it worked, knew how it felt to have her heart slam against her ribs and her mouth go dry.

She'd fallen in love before.

Probably more than once.

But there was something different about the way she felt when she was with Dallas. It was both comforting and exciting, familiar and completely new.

"True," she managed to say, her heart in her throat.

"When this is over, I'll take you to my favorite running trail."

"That sounds…" Dangerous? Foolish? Like something she shouldn't do? "Nice."

"Challenging is more like it, but you're in great shape. You won't have any trouble." He'd reached her side, his arm brushing hers as he opened the stairwell door. She felt it like a warm fire on a cold winter day.

They were standing so close, she could see his eyes gleaming through the darkness, and if she'd wanted to, she could have reached out and touched his shoulder again.

"Ready?" he asked, and her pulse jumped.

"For what?"

"You were going to the kitchen, right?"

Right! She'd just gotten a little sidetracked, a little distracted.

"Yes." She stepped past him, telling herself to do

what she'd been planning—walk down to the kitchen alone.

But he was there, and she couldn't resist him.

"Since we're both awake," she said, standing on the threshold and eyeing him through the darkness, "why don't you come, too?"

"I'm not much in the mood for conversation."

"I'm not, either."

"Then what do you have planned?"

"Jazz says that hot chocolate solves most of life's problems," she responded, her voice light, her pulse racing. She shouldn't be doing this. She knew it. It was one thing to spend time with Dallas because she had to. It was another to invite him to the kitchen for a cup of hot chocolate.

"Does she?"

"She says a lot of things when she's awake."

"You're worried about her." Another statement, but she nodded.

"We've been best friends for years. She's the only family I have."

"You have Zane."

"I should have said the only adult family," she clarified.

"You also have me and my folks." He flicked on the stairwell light, the single bulb casting a soft yellow glow across his hard features. He hadn't shaved in a couple of days, and the beginning of a beard shadowed his jaw.

She wanted to run her hand over it, feel its prickly softness. She turned instead, heading downstairs, the tread creaking. "It's not the same," she responded quietly. "I've never met your parents, and you're only here to make sure Zane is safe."

"You don't know me very well if you think that," he responded. No heat or anger in his voice. Just a statement that she could have ignored if she'd wanted to.

"I don't want you to feel obligated, Dallas."

"Obligated to Zane or to you?"

"Either." She'd reached the bottom of the stairs, and she stepped into the kitchen, a light over the sink casting long shadows through the room. "I asked you for help because I was desperate to keep Zane safe, but that doesn't mean—"

"Don't," he said so quietly she almost didn't hear.

"What?"

"Don't pretend that you think things are going to go back to the way they were after this is over."

"I wasn't pretending anything. I was just saying that Zane is my responsibility. Not yours or your parents."

"To me," he replied, the words rough and a little angry, "family means responsibility to each other."

"You're angry." She pulled out a small saucepan and grabbed the ingredients for hot chocolate. She didn't want any. She doubted he did. But she needed to occupy her hands. If she didn't, she might reach for him. She might try to smooth the frown line from between his brows or massage the tension from his shoulders. She might do any one of a dozen things that could get her into more trouble than she was already in.

"I'm irritated," he corrected. "We've spent a lot of time together—"

"I've noticed," she murmured, and his scowl deepened.

"I see."

"See what?" She poured milk into the pan but didn't turn the burner on.

"This isn't about Zane. It's about you."

"It's about both of us."

"You and Zane?"

"And me and you," she replied.

"Meaning?"

"I don't want any of us to be disappointed," she answered.

"You're assuming that's what's going to happen."

"Isn't it usually? Boy meets girl. They fall in love and then out of it. Everyone involved is hurt and disappointed."

"Love isn't a thing to fall into. It's an action. It's not a feeling. It's a choice."

"Those are nice words, Dallas, but when push comes to shove, most people love themselves more than they can ever love anyone else. When they have to choose between their own needs and the needs of the people they supposedly love, they always choose themselves."

"Most people? Or the people that you've known?"

"Most people I've known," she corrected, looking straight into his gorgeous eyes.

"I guess you haven't known many of the right people," he responded. He was still irritated or angry or whatever word he wanted to put to it. She could see that in the tightness of his jaw, the simmering heat in his gaze.

She wanted to tell him that she knew beyond a shadow of a doubt that he would always put the needs of the people he loved ahead of his own.

She should have told him, but his cell phone buzzed and the opportunity was lost.

He dragged it from his pocket, glanced at the caller ID and frowned.

"Is something wrong?"

"It's Brett." His voice was still gruff with emotion, his expression hard as he pressed a button and set the phone on the counter.

"It's Dallas," he said. "You're on speakerphone, Brett. Carly is with me. Is everything okay?"

"Finally! I've been trying to get in touch with her for ten minutes!"

"I didn't have my phone with me," Carly explained.

"You're out without a phone at three in the morning?"

She ignored the censure in his voice and the question. "Is Jazz okay?"

"Better than okay. She's started to come around. She opened her eyes a couple of minutes ago, when I asked her to. She squeezed the nurse's hand. She moaned. They've called the neurologist. He'll do a full assessment when he gets here, but this is great news, Carly. It looks like my Jasmine is coming back to me!"

"Coming back to all of us," she said, and he sighed.

"Let's not bicker over words."

"I wasn't bickering. I was just—"

"I'm sure Jazz would love to have you here as she's returning to consciousness," he said, cutting her off. "When can I expect you?"

She glanced at Dallas.

He shook his head.

Obviously, he didn't want her to go.

She was going anyway. "As soon as I can get there."

"A time frame would be nice. I'd like to take a shower, make myself a little more presentable for when she is really back."

"I can be there—"

"No," Dallas interrupted.

"What's that supposed to mean?" she hissed.

"It means, you're not going."

"Of course I am. She's my best friend."

"Hello?" Brett said. "I'm still here."

"I'll be at the hospital as soon as I can," Carly responded, running for the stairs and up to her room. She grabbed her coat and her purse, kissed Zane's forehead and straightened his covers. She didn't bother brushing her hair or putting on makeup, and she didn't bother checking in with Dallas again.

She was going to the hospital whether he liked it or not.

She stepped back into the hall, closing the door gently and heading for the front stairs. She expected to see Dallas there, blocking her path, insisting that she do things his way. Instead, he was at the front door, coat on, hands tucked into his pockets. He watched as she approached, his expression neutral.

"This is a mistake," he said when she reached him.

"Why?"

"Because, they could be watching the hospital. They could know she's waking up. They could be waiting somewhere on the road, knowing that you won't be able to stay away."

"They haven't tried to contact me in nearly a week. I think they've moved on to some other victim. Even if they haven't, I have to be there for Jazz."

"I'm not going to argue, Carly, because I know how it feels to wait for news about someone you love. I've already talked to Chance and Jackson. They'll stay with Zane. Just in case."

"In case what?"

"In case the people who are blackmailing you are

waiting for an opportunity to gain access to your son. Two people are a lot more difficult to overpower than one. Boone will meet us at the hospital." He opened the door, stepping outside before she could. His coat wasn't buttoned, and she could see his holster beneath it, see the butt of the gun he almost always carried when they went out.

"Ready?" he asked, just like he had in the house. Only this time, he held out his hand, and she took it, hurrying along with him as he jogged to his SUV, opened the door and let her in.

The streets of DC were quiet at this time on Sunday morning. Dallas was glad for that.

He wasn't glad they were on the way to the hospital. The move was too predictable, Carly's need to be with her friend too easily foreseen by anyone who might be interested. What the enemy could predict, he could prepare for. Dallas could have refused to drive Carly, but she'd have resented that. Knowing her, she'd have tried to find another way to get there. He'd have done the same if it were his friend in the hospital.

No. Not just a friend.

Carly's only adult family.

That was what she'd said.

He could admit that had stung.

They'd spent more time together in the past week than he'd spent with anyone in a long time. He'd escorted her to and from work. He'd watched her cut and polish gems, listened to her interact with people at the museum. He'd learned the cadence of her voice and the graceful way she moved.

"I wonder if she's really waking up," Carly said,

glancing at her phone for what had to be the twentieth time in as many minutes. "I texted Brett before we left, but he hasn't responded."

"We'll be at the hospital in five minutes. You'll be able to see for yourself then."

"I'd rather be at the hospital now," she muttered, leaning forward and peering through the windshield as if that could get them where they were going faster.

"If I had a teleporter, you could be," he responded, flicking on the wipers to brush away a few flakes of snow that were falling. The hospital campus was just ahead, and he scanned the road as he approached. Nothing. No cars idling on the side of the road. No shadows lurking near the edge of the road. He wasn't surprised.

Things had been quiet since Zane and Carly moved to his place. No emails, texts or phone calls. No kidnapping attempts or veiled threats. It was possible Carly was right. Maybe the blackmailer had been scared off. Or scared into approaching another victim, finding someone else he could use.

Dallas wanted to think that was the case.

He wanted to believe that Carly and Zane were out of danger.

He didn't.

This felt personal. He and the team had discussed it. They'd dug through all the information Carly had provided.

He hadn't mentioned it to her, hadn't asked if she knew anyone who might gain from her downfall, but he and the team had been discussing it. Chance and Jackson's sister Trinity had been doing some research, looking for connections that might give them a lead to follow.

So far, they'd come up empty.

On the surface, it seemed that Carly was exactly what she appeared to be—a hardworking single mother who was doing her best to care for her son. There'd been articles and write-ups on the work she did, but she had no website, no online presence. The freelance jobs she'd gotten had been obtained by word of mouth. She was at the point in her career where people sought her out. She didn't seek them. She was that good.

At least, that was what some of her former clients had said when Trinity had called and spoken to them. Carly's coworkers at the Smithsonian spoke highly of her, too. Carly was well liked and respected by the team of jewelry specialists she worked with.

He could understand why. He'd watched her work on a gemstone for three days, carefully crafting it to match one missing from an ornate antique necklace that was worth over a million dollars. He'd seen her place the stone in the necklace dozens of times, take it out, work it some more. She'd documented everything, taking pictures, writing notes, leaving a paper trail of her work so that a hundred years from now, anyone who encountered the piece would know exactly which stone was a replacement, who had cut it, what methods had been used.

The work was important to her. He could see that in the way she did it, but her coworkers respected her for more than that. She had an innate kindness, a way of dealing with problems in a respectful but straightforward manner. She didn't pull punches, but she didn't glory in her victories.

She was beautiful, too.

He'd be lying if he said he hadn't noticed that.

But it wasn't her beauty that intrigued him.

It was her smile, her humor, her easy way of interacting with everyone she met. It was the hard edge beneath the smooth surface. The hint of sorrow behind the smile. He'd learned a lot about her, and he wanted to know more.

That surprised him.

Lila had been his first real love. He'd met her at church after he'd left the military. She'd been funny and bright and interesting. He'd fallen for her about as fast and hard as anyone could. In the years since she'd passed away, he hadn't dated. Friends had tried to hook him up, but he'd refused invitations and not-so-subtle hints.

He'd wanted nothing to do with the dating scene, nothing to do with their efforts. Nothing to do with loving and losing and hurting again.

But Carly would be worth the risk.

She'd be worth the effort.

If she decided she was willing to take the chance.

He wasn't going to push. He wasn't going to force things. There was no hurry, no rush, no need to grasp for something that seemed about as inevitable as the rising tide or the setting sun. They were being drawn together. He could feel it, and he knew she could, too. What that meant, what they would allow it to mean, was something else entirely.

A car pulled in behind him, lights flashing in his rearview mirror. Not there. Then there.

It was behind him now, moving in close, nearly hugging his bumper.

"What's wrong?" Carly asked, shifting in her seat and peering out the back window.

"Probably nothing," he responded, but it felt like something. It felt like they were being stalked.

"Then why do you look like it's something?"

"I like to be prepared. Just in case."

The hospital parking garage was straight ahead, and he coasted to the ticket counter, unrolled his window and pressed the button to open the gate. He grabbed the ticket, eyeing the other car in the side-view mirror.

The windows were tinted probably a couple of shades darker than the law allowed. No license plate on the front. It looked like a new vehicle, and he figured either the owner was waiting for the tags to arrive, or it had been stolen from a dealership.

He pulled through the open gate, watching as the car behind him did the same.

Thousands of people visited the hospital. This could be anyone, but he had that feeling that had kept him alive on more than one occasion. The one that made the hair on his arms stand up, that made his body hum with adrenaline. The one that told him things weren't what they seemed to be, that danger was closing in.

"I wonder if Jazz will be scared when she realizes where she is. I wonder if she'll remember what happened," Carly said, but she was still looking out the back window. She sensed what he did—trouble.

The parking lot was quiet and nearly empty, but it was a closed area, difficult to maneuver through quickly. He wanted to be out in more open space when he stopped. A few witnesses would be nice, too.

"I think we'll go to the emergency entrance instead of parking here," he said, keeping his tone neutral. No sense in alarming Carly more than she already was.

"Because you think we're being followed?"

"I don't know if we're being followed. I just know that I don't want to take a chance."

"Good. Neither do I," she responded as he headed for the parking garage's exit ramp. He used the ticket to open the gate, pulling through it as headlights appeared at the top of the ramp. The car was following them. Just like he'd known it would.

"Call Sergeant Wright. Tell her we've got some trouble at the hospital. No license plate. It's a new Ford SUV. Dark blue. Tinted windows. Chrome hubcaps. Four doors."

She made the call as he sped around the side of the hospital, following the signs for the emergency entrance. There would be people there. A security guard at the door, staff, patients—if they made it there—

A car zipped out from a side street, blocking his path.

He slammed on the brakes and spun to the right, running up over the curb, bottoming out the car.

"Get down!" he shouted as the side window exploded in a hailstorm of shattered glass.

NINE

She didn't think getting down was going to keep her safe.

She did it anyway, shouting information into the phone, certain that Sergeant Wright was asking questions. Carly could hear the words, but the only thing that was registering was the slightly frantic edge to the police officer's voice. If she was scared, there was a good reason for Carly to be terrified. And she was. A series of pops. More shattering glass. Those sounds were a backdrop to Carly's racing heart and galloping pulse. Sirens. A car engine revving. She heard those and then silence.

"Don't move," Dallas growled.

He got out of the car and was back in it before she could think up a plan and act on it. The car moved, bumping off the curb, speeding away, cold air and snow streaming through the shattered window.

Carly straightened and caught a glimpse of the car that had pulled out in front of them. Engine still running, exhaust pouring from its tailpipe. Driver's door open, a body lying beside it.

Dead. She was nearly certain of that.

"Stay down!" Dallas demanded, his voice calm and cold as ice.

Snowflakes were falling now, drifting lazily in the headlights. She could feel them swirling into the car, landing on her neck and cheeks, and sliding down her cold skin. She shuddered, pulling her hood up over her hair. She could still feel the flakes, hear the swish of tires on the slushy road. She noticed that, and the tail-lights in front of her.

"I said, stay down," Dallas repeated, and she realized she was still upright, the phone in her hand, someone speaking, the cadence of the words quick and steady.

"Carly," Dallas warned, his hand sliding up her neck, his palm pressing lightly against the back of her head.

And she finally made herself move, ducking down, pressing the phone to her ear again.

She still couldn't hear. Her heart was beating too loudly in her ears, the sound of it blocking out whatever the sergeant was saying.

She could feel the car accelerate, though, the wind whistling through the shattered window.

"I've got the license plate number of a vehicle the police need to stop. It's the one that followed us into the garage," Dallas said, and she managed to hear that loud and clear.

He said the number. She tried to repeat it. Failed and tried again.

Finally, he grabbed the phone, gave the number quickly and handed it back to her.

"Tell her that the car exited at the ramp to 50 east. We're not following. I shot out one tire. They shouldn't get very far on it," Dallas said.

She repeated the information, her phone line suddenly

silent. Either the sergeant had disconnected, or Carly's phone had dropped the call.

She didn't bother calling back. She wasn't sure she could. Her hands were trembling, her muscles quivering with the need to move, to run. Away from the danger. Home to Zane. Back two months to the very first email she'd received. She should have called the police then. She should have trusted them and God instead of relying on herself.

She should have listened when Dallas said that going to the hospital was a mistake. She should have told him how much he was beginning to mean to her when she'd had the chance, because the way things looked, she may have missed her last opportunity.

Should have.

Could have.

Would.

If she had another chance.

Please, God. Get us out of this, she prayed silently.

She shuddered, jumping as Dallas's cell phone rang. He pushed a button on the dashboard, and Chance's voice filled the vehicle.

"Where are you?" he demanded, a clipped note to his tone that Carly had never heard before.

"If you didn't already know, you wouldn't be calling," Dallas responded.

"Maybe I should have asked what you think you're doing. You got a stand-down order from the police sergeant in charge of this case, Dallas. Why are you still in pursuit?"

"We're not."

"That's not what the sergeant seems to think."

"She's thinking wrong, then."

"Are either of you injured?"

"No."

"The perp who shot at you?"

"Probably dead. Since there was another vehicle with another perp inside, I didn't wait around to figure it out."

"You gave the police a description of the second vehicle?"

"Yes."

"Where are you headed now?"

"Not back to my place. I have a feeling this isn't over, and I don't want Zane in the middle of it."

"Drive to headquarters. I'll have people there ready to meet you."

"The streets are too narrow in the city, and traffic is going to pick up. I'm on the highway, heading northwest. Can you send someone out this way?"

"Yes."

Carly eased up, waiting for him to bark the orders for her to get down again. But he didn't say anything.

There were only a few other vehicles on the road, all of them passing in the fast lane. Dallas kept a steady speed, his eyes fixed on the road, his hands loose on the steering wheel. Snow was falling harder now, splattering against the windshield and coating the pavement.

He finished his conversation with Chance, disconnected the call.

"You're quiet," he said, his expression hard in the light from the dashboard.

"I'm worried about Zane."

"They weren't after Zane tonight."

"No. I guess they weren't, but what if they try to grab him while we're out here?"

"Chance and Jackson are with him. No one will be able to." He paused, then continued. "Are you sure the blackmailers are only trying to get you to cooperate with a forgery scheme, Carly?"

"What else would they be doing?"

"Trying to get revenge?"

"For what?"

"Only you can answer that."

"My answer is I haven't done anything to anyone. There's nothing for anyone to seek revenge for."

"You're very good at what you do. That's bound to cause jealousy."

"In my circle? Probably not. Gemstone cutting is an art, and it's not one that we get lots of credit for."

"You get paid well for what you do. I'm sure there are other people who'd have liked to have the job with the Smithsonian."

"Anyone with my skills would love a job like the one I have. But who I work for and what I make isn't something I advertise."

"The information is easy to find. If you know how to look for it."

"Meaning you looked?" She wasn't angry. She wasn't even really surprised. She'd done her research, too. She knew what HEART did. She knew they traveled the world, looking for the lost and bringing them home. She also knew they were incredibly good at finding what they were looking for.

"A coworker at HEART did."

"I see."

"I doubt it," he said, easing off the gas and glancing in the rearview mirror.

"Then maybe you should explain it to me," she countered.

"We're not sure the jewelry collection you're working on is the real target. We think you may be."

"When you say target, you mean victim. And when you say you're not sure, you mean you're pretty confident."

"Something like that," he admitted, offering the half smile that was becoming too familiar and too welcome.

"I don't have any enemies, Dallas. If that's what you're thinking, you can stop."

"Not all of our enemies are known. Sometimes, people we think are friends are actually foes."

"Not in my life."

"Don't close yourself off to the idea. This feels personal. I think that. Everyone on my team thinks it."

"I've been asked to create a bunch of stones that could imitate several very expensive pieces of jewelry. Cheap metal. Cheap gems. The antiques replaced, then sold on the black market. I showed you the pieces in the collection, Dallas. The stones I was supposed to be cutting and polishing were the exact sizes and cuts as the stones in those antiques. That's not personal. It's fact. And I'd say the 'request' was motivated by greed."

"If that were the only goal, it would be over. Once the police got involved, your blackmailer would have backed off."

"Which brings us right back to where the conversation started," she admitted.

"It brings us to what I need you to do—spend some time thinking about the people you know. Would any of them have anything to gain if you weren't around?"

"If I were dead, you mean?"

"Dead. In jail. On the run. Any of those could have happened if things had played out the way your blackmailer wanted."

"No one would gain anything from any of those scenarios."

"Do you have life insurance?"

"You mean you didn't already find out?"

"We have note of a policy, but not the amount."

"I do. For Zane's sake. He's the beneficiary."

"And who will his guardian be if something happens to you?"

Jazz, of course.

She couldn't say it. Could not make herself fill the silence with what he wanted to hear.

"She would never hurt me or Zane," she finally managed, and he glanced her way. Just a quick, searing look that made her breath catch.

"I hope you're right."

"She was attacked, Dallas!"

"Okay." That was it. No argument. No explanation. Just that one word that made her blood boil, because it sounded the same as *believe what you want to, but I know the truth.*

"I can't believe you think she would do something like that—fake an attempted kidnapping, have someone attack her. She could have died!"

"She's a children's book author. Is there good money in that?"

"Enough that she doesn't need to kill me for Zane's inheritance," she snapped. "Besides, her father died in a work accident when she was six. Her mother filed a wrongful death suit and won. Jazz doesn't have to work. She does because she enjoys it."

"You're sure about that?"

"Of course I am!"

"If she's so well-off, why's she living with you? Why not get her own place?"

"Her mother set up trusts with her husband's estate that were to be dispersed when Jazz turned twenty-five. When that birthday came and went, Mrs. Rothschild still didn't want to give up control. When Jazz moved in with me, she was in the middle of a legal fight to gain control of her part of the settlement. It took a few years. Eventually, she did, but by that time, she'd become such a big part of Zane's life that neither of us could imagine her moving out."

"Okay," he said in another tone that got her hackles up.

"What's that supposed to mean?"

"That I'll have Trinity check things out."

"Is she a member of HEART?" If so, Carly hadn't met her yet.

"She's Chance and Jackson's sister, a computer forensic expert, and the one person I know who can dig up everything there is to know about anyone."

"She doesn't have to dig around in Jazz's life. We've been friends since college. I know her as well as I know myself. I knew her when she was short on cash, and I can tell you she isn't short on it now. She's planning a huge New Year's Eve wedding. Five hundred guests. A gorgeous gown. You don't do that if you're broke."

"Some people do," he pointed out, and she frowned.

No way was he going to plant seeds of doubt in the garden of her confidence.

"I know Jazz," she repeated. "She doesn't want or need my life insurance policy. Period. End of story."

"Maybe not her, then. Maybe someone else."

"Who could there possibly be? My dad died from alcohol-related liver disease when I was in college. My mom is probably still living in a hoarder house, popping pills to make herself feel better about life, but I don't know, because she packed up after my father died, left town and never sent me her new address." She bit her lip, appalled at what she'd just said and the way she'd said it, all her anger and frustration spilling out into a short diatribe about people she hadn't seen in fifteen years.

He didn't comment, and the silence seemed filled with all the things he could have said.

"I know that sounded terrible," she finally said.

"It sounded honest."

"I know, but I feel like I need to explain why I sound the way I do when I talk about them."

"Not to me, you don't. My birth parents weren't exactly winners at life. I can understand the way you feel, and I know all about bitterness and anger, and the way they can rear their ugly heads when we least expect it. Neither of us can change where we came from, but we can make sure the place we're in is safe and happy and good for us. I know you love Jazz. I know she's family to you, but just think about what I said about the money, okay?"

She almost said no. Point-blank. Absolutely not. Never going to happen.

But Zane...

He had to be first. Always. She couldn't risk something happening to him because she'd stubbornly refused to look at the situation from a different angle.

"Okay."

"Thanks." He glanced her way again, offered a sweet smile that made her pulse jump. He was the knight in shining armor that so many women searched for and never found, but she wasn't a damsel in distress. She was a woman who'd made her own way, done her own thing, created a good life from the ashes of an old and difficult one. She didn't need him, but she wanted him around. That made her as vulnerable as she was strong.

"Do me another favor, will you?" he asked.

"That depends on what it is."

"Text Chance. Tell him that car I gave him a description of circled around and is behind us. Either that or we've got another tail. We're in Maryland. He'll need to call the local authorities for this. Sergeant Wright will be out of jurisdiction."

"What?" She swiveled in her seat, eyeing the snowy road and the headlights behind them. "Are you sure?"

"Yes."

"I need an exit number or something."

"He should be able to track my phone signal. We've got GPS attached and a system set up. He just needs to turn it on."

She did what he asked, fingers fumbling as she sent the info, her attention on the headlights that seemed to be keeping a steady distance. For now.

"What are we going to do?"

"Exit the freeway. See if we can find a safe place to go to ground until help arrives."

"I'm not sure I like that plan."

"Do you have a better one?"

"Hot chocolate?" she muttered.

He patted her knee, his hand warm and comforting. "It's going to be okay."

"I'm glad one of us thinks so," she responded as they exited the freeway and headed farther away from the city.

Dallas kept his distance because of Carly.

If he'd been alone, he'd have pulled off the road, cut the lights and staged an ambush.

Instead, he crawled along a backcountry road, looking for a safe place to pull off. The snow was a good camouflage, swirling through the predawn darkness, tinging the world gray and white. Up ahead, an old church jutted up against the landscape, its steeple crisp white. No lights. No people. No safe place to leave Carly while he went after the perp.

He could see the headlights a quarter mile behind, there and then gone as he took a curve in the road.

This was the opportunity he'd been waiting for, and he took it, coasting off the road and onto a dirt driveway edged by hay fields. He drove a hundred yards in and switched off the car.

"What are we doing?" Carly whispered, as if she were afraid her voice would carry all the way to the other car.

"Waiting."

"For?"

"The car to pass or help to arrive. Whichever comes first."

"What if it doesn't pass?"

"It will." And then it would circle back around. He didn't bother mentioning that. Carly would have no trouble figuring it out on her own.

"Do you think it's the car you shot at?"

"If it is, he's come a long way on a flat tire." And, hopefully, he wouldn't be able to go much farther.

"Chance texted me." She glanced at her phone, the screen glowing in the darkness.

"Put that away," he said, shifting in his seat so he had a clear view of the road.

She did as he asked, tucking the phone into her pocket. "He says he's contacted the local police. Boone is about four miles behind us. He says don't do anything stupid."

He would have laughed if he weren't so frustrated.

If he were alone...

But he wasn't.

Carly's safety was his priority. Getting the perp was secondary.

Headlights flashed on the pavement and the car crept past. Limped past?

It was definitely driving on a flat tire, bumping along at slow-speed.

Dallas expected it to return quickly.

When it didn't, he opened his door.

"Stay in the car," he said, stepping out into the snowy morning. He walked to the road, using the field as cover. A second car approached, passing almost as slowly as the first. Not Boone. He'd have used the tracking system to locate Dallas's car.

He waited in the shadows, watching as the vehicle continued up the road, turning into what must have been the church parking lot. Was he meeting the perp? Giving him a ride back?

It didn't matter.

Dallas's hands were tied until backup arrived.

He made his way back to the car and climbed in.

"I texted Chance and let him know the guy passed us," Carly said. "I also texted Brett. He wanted to know where I was. I guess Jazz woke up enough to ask for me and Zane."

"What'd you tell him?"

"That we had car trouble, and I'd be there as soon as I could. He offered to send a friend of Jazz's to come pick us up. I told him we had things under control."

"Good. I'd rather you not tell any of your contacts where we are."

"I'd rather not be where we are."

"That, too," he agreed, pulling a blanket from the back of the car and tossing it around her shoulders. The broken window allowed wind and snow to blow in, and she was shivering, her teeth chattering from the cold.

"Thanks," she said, offering a smile that made his heart ache for all the things he'd thought he would never want again.

"Oh. I almost forgot," she said. "Boone is nearly here. He said he could see the church."

"Good." That was exactly what he'd been hoping for. "Stay here." He stepped out of the car again.

"What are you doing?"

"I'm going to the church. I think the perp is meeting someone there. He probably got tired of following us on a flat tire. He's getting a new ride."

"I hope you're kidding, Dallas."

"I never kid about things like this." He reached over the seat, grabbed the duffel he always kept there. He'd learned young to prepare for anything. It was a lesson that had served him well over the years.

He pulled out leather gloves and a wool cap and put both on. He had a blanket folded in the bottom of the duffel, and he pulled it out, setting it on the console as he checked his Glock, making sure it was fully loaded.

"Dallas, I really don't think this is a good idea," Carly said, watching as he tucked the gun back in its holster.

"It's the only one I've got, so we're going with it."

"We can wait for Boone and the police and the cavalry. We can wait for Christmas to come, for all I care."

"We'll freeze before that happens."

"Dallas…" She shook her head.

"What?"

"I don't want anything to happen to you."

"What could possibly happen?"

"You could die?" She looked scared, and for a split second, he considered waiting for Boone, but he could hear a car engine. He knew that backup was minutes away.

"Don't worry. I've survived a lot worse situations."

"Not when I knew you," she replied, grabbing his hand and looking straight into his eyes. "If you die, no amount of hot chocolate will make it better."

"I won't. I'll be back as soon as I get a look at the perp."

"Who says you'll be able to do that? By the time you reach his car, he'll be gone."

Not if Dallas shot a few more tires out while he drove away. He hadn't trained as a sharpshooter for nothing.

"Stay in the car," he said again, and then he did what he'd been wanting to do for nearly a week. He leaned in and kissed her. He meant it to be quick and gentle and sweet. A friendly reminder that everything really would be okay.

It was more than that.

So much more than what he expected. Maybe even more than what he wanted.

Lights splashed on the road, tires crunching over snow and pavement.

Boone arriving, and Dallas was still at the car, staring into Carly's eyes, trying to figure out how he'd gone from not knowing her at all to feeling like he'd never really known anyone else.

He stepped back, closed the door and walked away from the car, the cold wind whipping at his face as he headed toward the old church and whatever trouble was waiting for him there.

TEN

Boone arrived seconds after Dallas left. Apparently, he thought he was going to do the same thing Dallas had. Leave her to go hunt for the bad guys. Only this time, she didn't plan to be left.

She climbed out of the car before he could walk away, following him into tall wheatgrass.

"I told you to stay in the car," he hissed.

"It's freezing in there."

"And it's not cold out here?" he responded, but he didn't seem nearly as determined to leave her as Dallas had been.

Dallas, whose kiss was still lingering on her lips.

She shoved the thought aside. Waiting wasn't something she'd ever been good at. She'd taught herself patience, because gemstone cutting demanded it. Moving too quickly could ruin a beautiful rough stone. Acting without planning could ruin a week of careful work. Any master gemstone cutter knew that the art of creating the perfect cut for a stone lay in the ability to work slowly, methodically and with precision. But sometimes Carly forgot just how important those things were in daily life.

Like right now, when she was following Boone through the field, heading toward the parking lot of the old church. Snow flew in her face, blinding her for a second.

And Boone was gone.

She whirled around, trying to spot him, and nearly screamed when he snagged the back of her coat.

"This way," he said without a hint of impatience in his voice. "If you want to come, keep up."

A light flashed to the left, and Boone pressed her down into a thick patch of brush.

"Down and stay there until I return," he commanded.

She was so surprised she did what he said without arguing, bobbing back up a moment later, because it was better to see what was coming than to hide. It was still there. A flashlight, she thought, the swirling snow dancing in its beam. It arced across the ground, as if the person holding it were searching for something, then disappeared again.

Was someone looking for tracks in the snow?

Evidence that others had come this way?

Aside from Chance and Boone, she could think of only one person who would be out there: the guy who'd been driving the other car.

Please, God, don't let him see me, she prayed silently as she eased deeper into the brush.

The light moved past, far enough away that the person carrying it was nothing but a black shape in the darkness. She tracked its movements until it went out. Was the person moving toward her or away?

She didn't know, and she didn't plan to wait around to find out. She eased across an overgrown churchyard, darting past an old swing set, its swings dusted in snow, their rusted chains creaking as they swayed in the wind.

Creepy.

But even creepier was the fact that she had no idea where the guy she'd seen had gone. She glanced around, searching for his light. It was gone, hidden by foliage or outbuildings.

Or turned off because he'd realized she was close and didn't want his movement tracked.

She shuddered.

A field of wheatgrass led to an old house, several more buildings visible in the distance. She stepped into the tall, dry grass, crouching to try to keep out of sight. That slowed her movements. It also made her less of a target for anyone who might have a gun and planned to use it.

Do you have life insurance?

Dallas's words were suddenly in her head, and she couldn't shake them. She'd told him there was no one who'd want to harm her, and she believed it, but they'd come after her tonight. Not Zane.

Did they plan to kidnap her and force her to make the gemstones they'd demanded?

It would be a lot easier to hire someone to do the job.

There weren't many people trained to use old methods and tools to make the cuts, but there were plenty of people who could use modern tools to do it. If the goal was simply to pass forged jewels off as real ones for long enough to get away with the million-dollar collection, using modern tools would work. Even a really good forgery would be spotted eventually once someone like Carly got her hands on it.

She'd known that all along—if they did what she'd

suspected they would and switched out the jewelry, she'd know immediately. She'd recognize her work, of course, but she'd also know that the settings weren't true antiques, that the metal was cheap. She'd worked with jewelry for a decade, and she had an eye for quality.

If that had happened, she'd have had to go to Michael, the police, explain what had happened. She'd probably be suspected of aiding and abetting. She'd known that, but she'd had no choice but to put her faith in the system, to believe that if she was suspected and investigated, she'd be exonerated.

Now, with Dallas's words ringing through her head, she couldn't help wondering if there'd been more going on than she'd suspected, if maybe this was about a personal vendetta, a bid to destroy her and her credibility, someone gaining from her death.

Not Jazz.

She couldn't believe that.

Wouldn't.

The wind blew through the field, rustling the grass and masking any sound of pursuit.

She didn't dare straighten and look around. She kept her head down, heading toward one of the outbuildings. It was farther than she'd realized, and she was cold. Freezing, really, the wind stinging her cheeks and stealing her breath. She stepped out of the grass and into what had once been an orchard, the gnarled trees dormant, their roots and branches entwined, creating a thicket that was nearly impossible to move through.

For once, Carly was glad for her small size. She squeezed between branches, ducked under them, the outbuilding still too far away. She thought about turning back, but she was afraid she'd run right into the person who was behind her.

She reached a fence that leaned so far inward it was barely standing. Chain link, no barbed wire. She stepped on it as she moved through, smashing it closer to the ground, her feet so numb she couldn't tell how much pressure she was using.

Somewhere behind her, a branch snapped, the sound sharp against the winter hush.

She darted forward, racing toward the barn, and suddenly realized her mistake. She was heading to the closest visible building. Which was exactly what 99.9 percent of people in her situation would do. She changed trajectory, running around the side of the barn, her feet like wooden logs attached to her ankles. Her lungs burned from the cold, and her hood had come down, snow sliding down her neck and soaking her T-shirt.

She passed a barn door that hung crooked on its hinges, slowing to try to catch her breath and think. She scanned the dark field beyond, spotted two other outbuildings poking up on the horizon. She could make it to one. Hopefully before her stalker caught up with her.

She jogged away, wishing she weren't leaving such clear tracks in the snow, hoping that her pursuer would assume she'd entered the barn and go in after her. She moved by rote, log feet tapping against the ground, thinking about winter and Christmas and how excited Zane was by it all.

She didn't realize her thoughts were drifting until she reached another chain-link fence. This one stood solid, six feet of metal rungs between her and the next outbuilding. Several trees grew close on either side of it, and she darted toward one, hoping she'd be hidden by the elm's thick trunk and drooping branches.

Focus! That was what she needed to do, because if she didn't, she'd be wandering around in the field until she was caught or she froze. It was bad enough to die at the hands of an enemy. To freeze to death in the middle of an abandoned field seemed even worse.

She started climbing, the tiny pebbles of glass in her mittens probably digging through flesh. She couldn't feel it. Her hands were numb. Her ears were numb. Her cheeks burned.

Someone grabbed the back of her coat, pulling her off the fence so quickly she didn't have time to react. She slammed into a hard chest, steel-like arms wrapping around her stomach and her shoulders, a hand slapping over her mouth.

She smelled leather and snow, and then she was on the ground, pressed into grass and dirt and ice. She fought. Or tried to, anyway. Her movements were clumsy, her body pinned by someone who was bigger and stronger than her.

She felt him shift, thought he might be reaching for a gun. She expected to feel metal pressed against her temple. Instead, she was pinned more thoroughly, her hands locked down at her sides, fingers around her wrist, body to body and thigh to thigh with someone. Lips grazing her ear, warm breath against cold skin.

"Stop," he growled.

One word, but she knew the voice, and she stilled, snow falling gently all around her. None of it landed on her, though, because Dallas was blocking it along with the wind. She blinked snow and ice from her lashes, and she could see him, his eyes blazing in the blue-gray darkness.

"I thought you were at the church," she whispered, and he covered her mouth again.

He didn't speak. He didn't have to.

He wanted her quiet, and she nodded to let him know she would be.

His hand slipped away, cold leather replaced by colder air. Then he was cupping her face with bare hands, his skin warm against her frozen cheeks and jaw.

She shivered, and he met her eyes, frowning but still not speaking, the warmth from his body and his hands seeping into her.

Somewhere to the left, a person was moving. She could hear feet on the frozen ground, feel the vibration of the fence beside her as whoever it was began to climb. Dallas moved subtly, hands sliding away, gloves back on, his body still covering hers.

They were hidden by darkness, thick grass and the shadow of the tree she was hiding behind, but a light flashed a few feet away. Every muscle in her body tensed, and Dallas's hand dropped to her mouth again. Just a whisper of a touch this time. A reminder to stay silent as the light bobbed along the ground a few feet away, dancing on the edges of frozen blades of grass. Moving closer with every frantic beat of her heart.

An owl hooted somewhere to the east. Boone. Dallas was certain of it. He'd been using the same signal for as long as they'd been working together, the soft owl cry a warning that he was nearby or that trouble was.

"That's Boone," he whispered in Carly's ear. "He must have finally arrived."

"He's been here for a while. We were together, and then he went looking for someone who was walking around with a flashlight."

"And you thought that was your signal to go it on your own?"

She didn't answer.

Which was for the best.

The perp was out there somewhere. The quieter they were, the better.

He searched for light, knowing the guy would turn it on again. There! Just like he'd expected. Carly's head moved, and he was certain she was watching the light, worried the perp was getting closer.

He wanted to tell her it would be okay, that Boone was there, that the police would arrive shortly. That the guy with the flashlight would be apprehended and they'd get the answers they needed, answers that would allow her to move on with her life.

But he didn't trust the wind to not carry his words, and the perp was close, moving on the other side of the fence, trying to figure out which direction Carly had gone.

The owl hooted again. Closer.

The perp must have noticed. His light went off, the area it had illuminated blue-gray with snow and darkness. Dallas could hear his footsteps, crunching through the grass, moving away. Probably toward one of the outbuildings.

Dallas pressed his lips close to Carly's ear, inhaling the scent of flowery shampoo as her loose hair brushed his nose and cheek.

"Do. Not. Move," he whispered, enunciating every

word. He eased away, standing and approaching the fence, peering through it, searching for the perp.

He was a hundred yards away, crossing the field, heading toward the closest barn.

Dallas whistled, the sound mimicking a chickadee's warning call.

The perp stopped, whirling back around and sprinting toward the fence line. It didn't seem like an aggressive run, but more scared. He went down, popped back up again and kept going, clambering back over the fence a hundred yards away.

Dallas could have taken him out. A warning, a gunshot, and the guy would be done, but he seemed more frantic than threatening as he headed back into the thicket of old orchard trees.

Seconds later, Boone stepped out of the darkness. Not there and then there, moving so silently Dallas wouldn't have known he'd appeared if Boone hadn't spoken.

"Should we go after him?"

"I think he's heading for the barn or the house. He's sure not going back to his car, and he can't stay out in the cold for much longer."

"He can do just about anything he wants, but a lot of what he might be planning could get him killed," Boone responded. "I parked at the church, took a look in his vehicle."

"See anything interesting?"

"A few papers sitting on the passenger seat. They might have blown out of the car when I opened the door, and I might have had to pick them up and stuck them in my pocket to get a better look at later."

"It's a good story, Boone. You planning on sticking

to that if those papers are something you'll need to turn in to the police?" Dallas reached for Carly's hand and pulled her upright.

"Probably not. Lying isn't something I make a habit of. Since the guy left his car door unlocked, I might argue that he was asking to be robbed and leave it at that."

"What was on the papers? Did you see anything?" Carly asked, her teeth chattering. Her cheeks had been ice-cold to the touch, her entire body shaking. She shouldn't have left the car, but telling her that wasn't going to change the fact that she had.

He slid out of his thick parka, dropping it around her shoulders as Boone shrugged and responded. "I took a quick look. One was a kid's drawing. The other looked like photos of some fancy-looking jewelry. Not sure about the third. Looked like a list of names, but I didn't recognize any of them."

"Jewelry?" Carly asked. "Old stuff?"

"Ma'am, you are asking the wrong person," Boone responded. "The only time I can tell the difference between old and new is when we're talking about batches of chocolate chip cookies or home-baked bread. So—" he met Dallas's eyes "—what's the plan?"

"We find him, figure out who he is, who sent him and why," Dallas said.

"That's exactly what I had in mind," Carly said. Even with his coat on, she was still shivering, her hair covered with snow that was melting and sliding down her face and neck.

He brushed some of it away, and she scowled.

"I'm fine," she said.

"I didn't ask."

"You were going to."

"I was also going to say that you were supposed to stay in the car, but I didn't. You have the Maglite I keep in the duffel?" he asked, and her scowl deepened.

"How did you know?"

"Because I know you're not the kind of person who likes to go into anything unprepared. Can I have it?"

She fished it out of her pocket and handed it to him. "Thanks."

"You can thank me by taking your coat and going after that guy. I'll stay here and wait for you so that I won't distract either of you from the hunt." There was a hint of sarcasm in her voice. He ignored it and the parka that she tried to shove into his hands.

"We're sticking together this time."

"Because you don't think I'll follow orders?"

"Because I think that the only way you're going to keep from freezing is by moving, and because until this guy is cuffed and in a patrol car, I don't want you by yourself out here." He dropped the coat around her shoulders again.

"You freezing isn't going to make me feel any better about the mess I've gotten myself into," she muttered.

"I'm in layers, boots and a fleece-lined shirt. You're not. And you didn't get into this mess. Someone threw you here. So how about we stop talking and get moving?" He grabbed her hand, pulling her along at a pace he hoped was quick enough to get her blood flowing.

Boone stayed beside them until they reached the edge of the orchard, then he motioned toward the house and the cars' headlights that were shining there. Two sets. No emergency lights, but Dallas was still almost certain they were police cruisers.

He signaled for Boone to check things out, then waited at the edge of the orchard. Carly stood beside him. Silent. Still. Having her with him was a risk. But leaving her alone was a bigger one.

He eyed the barn that stood a couple of hundred yards away. The door hung crookedly, swinging rhythmically. As if someone had entered or exited recently.

There were no windows on this side of the structure, no way for the perp to scan for trouble except through the cracks in the walls and doors.

The barrel of a gun could fit through any one of those openings.

To the left, the remains of an old Ford truck sat on crumbling concrete, the wheels on one side gone, the vehicle listing heavily.

If he were on the run and hiding, he wouldn't take shelter in the most obvious place. He'd hide in a place like that truck. He'd wait until the people who were pursuing him went into the barn, and then he'd slip out and disappear.

He crouched, pulling Carly down with him.

"I'm going to check the truck," he said. "It should only take me a couple of minutes. I want you to stay here. Just like this. Low to the ground and quiet."

"The barn door is moving. He's probably in there," she whispered, her voice so quiet he barely heard.

"Would you hide in there?" he asked, pulling the edge of his coat together and zipping it up. She might not be shaking, but she still looked cold, her cheekbones nearly white in the dim light.

"I…" She eyed the barn and then the truck. "I'd probably hide in the truck and hope everyone else went in the barn."

"Exactly," he said.

She smiled. "Be careful, Dallas."

"I don't know how to be anything else," he joked, but her smile had fallen away, and she was studying his face, her gaze touching his cheeks, his hair, his jaw.

"It would be easier if you looked like Josh," she said quietly.

He didn't ask what she meant. He knew.

If he'd looked like Josh, it would be easier to remind herself of the past, of the disappointments, of the heartbreaks. It would be easier to keep her distance, keep her emotions in check, guard whatever part of herself she kept hidden from the world.

But she was right. He and Josh had been half brothers. Different hair color, different build, different jawline and cheekbones and mouth. The only physical trait they had shared were their eyes. Both of them had bluish eyes, but Josh had been fair, like his father. Dallas had been darker, like his.

"Stay here, and stay down," he said, skimming his gloved finger along the line of her jaw and then turning away, because he had to.

They both needed time to figure things out, and they wouldn't get that until Carly had her life back.

First things first.

He could almost hear his mother's singsong voice ringing through the hushed winter morning. "Adoptive mother" was what people liked to say when they were talking about his relationship with Sarah Morgan, but he didn't think of her that way.

She was the person who'd signed him up for his first day of high school and insisted on walking into the building with him to make sure no one bothered him.

He'd acted like he didn't want her there, but he'd been secretly amused that a five-foot-nothing, ninety-pound woman was trying to protect him. Amused and pleased.

She'd been the one to take him tux shopping for his senior prom, who'd helped him choose a corsage for his date. She'd been to every one of his sporting events from the time he was thirteen until he'd left home for college. She'd sent him care packages when he'd been in the dorm and when he'd joined the military. She'd sat by his bed for days after the accident, and he'd never once seen her cry while she was there.

He'd seen the tears drying on her cheeks, though, and he'd held her hand at Lila's memorial service. He'd patted her back, told her he'd be okay and made himself be, because he couldn't stand to break her heart again. Currently, she and his father were on an anniversary cruise, sailing around the Caribbean to celebrate their fortieth year together. They'd be back in two days, and he'd have to tell them about Zane and Carly.

He wanted it to be good news that wasn't tainted with anything ugly or hard.

He wanted Zane safe and Carly happy and all of them meeting under good circumstances without several HEART members standing guard.

First things first.

Right now, he had a perp to catch.

He slipped into the shelter of the old trees, moving in the deep shadow of the tree line as he headed toward the truck and whoever might be waiting for him there.

ELEVEN

Carly crouched in the shadow of the trees, watching as Dallas crept toward the truck. If she hadn't been able to see him, she wouldn't have known he was there. He moved soundlessly. No snapping twigs or rustling grass. Like a wraith, he seemed to glide across the frozen ground. Not running or jogging, just moving with a kind of graceful ease she envied.

In the distance, a car door slammed, and voices carried through the snowstorm.

Boone must have reached the police.

Were they heading toward the barn?

She thought about texting to let him know where Dallas was, but she was afraid the light on her cell phone would give her location away. Instead, she rooted herself to the ground, her feet completely numb, her legs leaden. Dallas's coat was warm, though, and she'd tucked her knees into it so that most of her body was covered.

Despite what he'd said, he had to be cold. The windchill was in the teens.

He didn't seem bothered by it, though. He moved at a slow, steady pace, walking parallel to the barn and the pickup, nothing more than one dark shadow among many.

And then he was gone.

Just like that.

One minute she could see him at the edge of the tree line, the next he'd disappeared into the landscape. She looked for movement, but the entire orchard was swaying, snow billowing from branches, the few dead leaves that had still been clinging to trees flying off.

An early-winter storm was what the meteorologist had said, a very small weather event.

If this was small, she'd like to see big.

Or maybe she wouldn't.

Like Zane, she loved the snow, but she didn't much care for sitting in the darkness, listening to the wind howl and wondering where Dallas had gone.

She shifted her gaze to the truck, her heart thundering as she saw movement there. The front passenger door had been closed before. Now it was cracked open, an unseen hand keeping it from slamming into a two-foot pile of stones or bricks that was just a foot away.

It had to be the driver of the car.

Either he'd seen the lights from the police cars, or he'd realized that no one was going into the barn. Whatever the case, it looked like he planned to run. A minute passed, and the door stayed open. Dallas didn't reappear, and the cold seeped through the soles of Carly's Keds, gnawing at her aching, frozen feet.

They hadn't been the best footwear choice, but then, she hadn't realized she'd be crouching outdoors for an hour during a snowstorm.

Not that it had been an hour. It felt like a lifetime, her legs cramping as she tried to stay in place, mind racing with a million things that might go wrong. Like Dallas getting hurt, getting shot, getting killed.

Suddenly, the truck door swung wide-open, and a man jumped out. He took off running, away from the headlights that were still shining near the house. Away from the road, the church, his car. And Dallas was right behind him, appearing from what seemed like nowhere, tackling the guy with so much force they both slid across the icy ground.

Acting without thought, Carly ran toward them, passing the truck and the pile of stones. Bricks, she realized as she grabbed one and ran toward Dallas. Halfway across the distance that separated them, she realized what she was doing, remembered his words about being a distraction and making it more dangerous for both of them.

She skidded to a stop, watching as Dallas yanked a much smaller man to his feet.

At least, she thought it was a man. She wasn't close enough to see features, and she had no idea if the person was male or female.

She thought he said something. To the perp, or maybe to her.

"Do you need help?" she called and then realized her mistake immediately.

Dallas glanced her way, his focus shifting for a split second, and in that tiny amount of time, the perp slammed his foot into Dallas's bad knee. Dallas went down hard.

Carly didn't wait to see if he'd get up again. She was already racing forward, barreling into the guy who'd kicked him. He grabbed her arm as they both fell, tumbling in a tangle of arms and legs and flying fists, the brick slipping from her fingers.

She'd learned to fight young, but the guy she was going against had no clue. He flailed with his right arm and then his left, never quite making contact. If he had a weapon, he didn't pull it, and when Dallas dragged Carly back and set her on her feet, the guy was still down, lying in a heap in melted snow, his gasping breaths cutting through the silence.

"Get up," Dallas ordered, something sharp and hard in his voice.

The guy didn't respond, and Dallas leaned down, grabbing him by the front of his coat and pulling him to his feet. There was something about his size, the width of his shoulders, the way he cocked his head to the side, ran his hand over his hair, that reminded her of...

"Michael?" she asked, so shocked she thought she had to be wrong. There was no way her friend, a man she'd known for a decade, a guy who'd put in a good word for her and gotten her a job at the Smithsonian, who'd always seemed like a perfect gentleman, a wonderful friend, a warm and loving human being, would do something like this.

She took a step toward him, wanting to get a closer look, to prove to herself that she was mistaken, because there was no way it was Michael Raintree. Not only was he too nice of a guy to plot evil things against her, but he had too much respect for antiquities to ever steal them.

"Don't," Dallas cautioned, his hand on her shoulder.

"I would never hurt her," Michael said, and his voice was the same soft baritone that she heard every day when he called to check on her progress on the collection, to ask if she needed anything, to tell her how wonderful it was that they finally had a chance to work together again.

"Tell that to someone who's going to believe it," Dallas growled, fury oozing out of every word.

"It's the truth. Carly and I have been friends for years. I respect her as an antiquities expert, and I like her as a person. I wouldn't do anything to…"

His voice trailed off, because he obviously realized he had done something. He'd apparently done a lot of things, and she could barely wrap her mind around that.

"It's complicated," he finally said, and Dallas snorted.

"You know what isn't complicated?" Dallas responded. "Loyalty. Friendship. Doing right by the people who trust you."

"You don't understand."

"Maybe you should explain, then," Carly said, her stomach churning, her heart sick. She didn't want to believe it was him, but the truth was right there in front of her.

"I…can't."

"You're going to have to, because the police are already here." Dallas gestured to several people who were walking across the field, flashlights in their hands. "And they're going to want to know."

"I can't," he repeated, and then he turned and tried to run.

Dallas dragged him back, yanking his arm up behind his back and holding it there.

"Don't hurt him," Carly said, and Dallas met her gaze, his eyes blazing.

"I don't hurt people for sport or revenge. And he's really fortunate that I don't. What weapons are you carrying, Michael?"

"None."

"Someone fired a gun from your car."

"It wasn't me."

"Then who was it?"

"I can't say."

"You won't say."

"Right now, they're the same thing." He sounded weary, and Carly couldn't help feeling sorry for him.

For a man who'd tried to kidnap Zane. Tried to set her house on fire. Hired people who'd hurt Jazz.

She turned away, sickened by all of it, the whole mess they were in.

She walked through the crunching, snow-covered grass, made her way past the police and Boone. She didn't look at any of them. She was too busy trying to hold back tears and telling herself she'd be a fool to cry for someone who didn't deserve it.

But Michael had a wife and children. They lived in a brownstone in the same neighborhood as Carly, had dinner together every few weeks and talked shop and kids and life. He was a deacon in his church, and his wife ran the church nursery program. They were the epitome of a loving Christian couple.

And then he'd done this and ruined it all.

"Carly!" someone called. She ignored the summons.

She had the key to Dallas's car, and this time she didn't have to crawl through the window. She opened the passenger door and climbed in, took the key from her pocket, shoved it in the ignition and started the car.

The air blowing from the vents was still cold, but she didn't care.

She needed to put some distance between herself and Michael. She sure didn't want to look in his face, listen to his voice, feel sorry for what he was going to lose because of what he'd done.

The driver's door opened, and Dallas climbed in.

She wanted to resent the fact that he'd come after her, that he'd felt the need to follow her, to offer—what? Comfort? Protection? Companionship? She didn't need those things, and she shouldn't want them. She should have told him she was fine, that he should go back to Michael and the police.

But she wasn't upset, resentful or even annoyed.

She was relieved that she didn't have to sit alone mulling over questions that had no answers.

So maybe she did need those things he always seemed to offer.

He lifted the blanket and tucked it around her shoulders, her knees and her feet, and he was so close she could see the stubble on his chin, smell coffee and leather on his skin. If it had been a little lighter, she would have been able to see the flecks of green and gold in his eyes, the deep, rich black of his hair.

"I'm sorry," he said, sincerely and with so much compassion, her throat clogged with tears.

"We've been friends since college," she replied, a tear somehow escaping, slipping down her cheek and mixing with the icy water that was dripping from her hair. "Aside from Jazz, he's the last person I would have suspected of something like this."

"He's not admitting anything to the police," he said. "He's told them he wants a lawyer."

"So he's not denying it, either." Her voice was husky with emotion. She could hear it, and she knew he could.

"No, but there would be no sense in that, would there? He's miles from home in a stolen car—"

"He stole the car?"

"Someone did, and he was the one driving it. I guess you can draw your own conclusion."

"You know what I'd rather do?" she said, another tear slipping down her cheek. She hated crying almost as much as she hated being betrayed by people she cared about.

"What?" He wiped moisture from her cheeks, pulled the blanket a little tighter around her shoulders.

"Go to the hospital to see Jazz, go back to your place and see Zane. Close my eyes and open them to find out all of this was a bad dream."

"Not a horrible nightmare?" he asked, and she found herself smiling.

"I guess I understated things a little."

"Once the police give us permission, I'll drive you to the hospital. If Jazz is awake, I'm sure she'll be as happy to see you as you will be to see her."

"So you've got no more suspicions about her?" she asked.

"Truth? I don't know."

"Michael as good as admitted to us that he was the one blackmailing me."

"He admitted involvement, but this operation has required a boatload of people. Either the network Michael is involved in is huge, or he's got a lot of money and he's tossing it at anyone who's willing to help him."

"Maybe it's both. Maybe it's neither." She still didn't want to believe that Michael was a criminal, but the evidence was right in front of her: the crumbling driveway, the police cars, the snow swirling through the still-dark night. "But he does know my schedule almost as well as Jazz. He also knows what school Zane attends, when he has the day off. When I'll be home and when I won't. He knows I'm a runner and that I follow a pretty rigid routine."

He knew all those things, and if she was honest with herself, she'd admit that he had more access to the details of her life than anyone, other than Jazz.

"He also knows you'd do anything for your son," Dallas commented.

"That, too. But…"

"What?"

"He seems like such a genuinely nice guy. I've never heard him raise his voice to anyone. He does his work well and efficiently. I've never heard anyone say a bad word about him."

"They're going to say plenty now," he said drily.

"Poor Mallory. She's going to be devastated."

"That's his wife, right?"

"Yes. They've been married for ten years, trying to have a second child for most of that time. They adopted a little boy six months ago, and they all seemed so happy." She sighed, squeezing the bridge of her nose and forcing back more tears.

There was nothing she could do about any of this. Michael had made his own mess. He'd have to clean it up and pay the consequences.

"She okay?" someone asked, and she realized she'd closed her eyes.

She opened them and saw Boone peering in the broken side window. "I'm fine."

"Maybe you are, but I brought you this anyway. Dallas asked me to grab one from the emergency supply I keep in my Jeep." He thrust something through the window, holding it out until she took it.

"Chocolate?" She eyed the candy, not sure why he'd

brought it to her. She sure wasn't hungry, and she didn't think she could swallow anything without choking.

"Chocolate solves most of life's problems," Dallas said, opening his door and getting out of the car. "What it doesn't," he continued as he pulled the key from the ignition and met her eyes, "time will."

The words were an exact repeat of what she'd said to him. Jazz's words, technically, but they sounded different coming from him.

They sounded like a promise, like a vow, like the sweetest whisper of the dearest friend and closest companion.

She blinked, still staring into his face and his eyes, but unable to speak, because his gesture wasn't showy or big or brilliant. It was quiet and small and sincere, and a tiny little part of her heart loved him for it.

"Thank you," she finally managed to say, and she wasn't sure if she meant the words for him or Boone or both.

Dallas nodded, closing the door and rounding the car. He spoke to Boone for a few seconds before opening her door and giving her a hand out.

"Boone's going to drive us to the local sheriff's office. Sergeant Wright will meet us there. Once we're interviewed and give our statements, we'll bring you to the hospital." He settled the blanket around her shoulders, pulled her hood up and tucked a few strands of hair beneath it.

"Thanks," she said again, and he took her free hand, squeezing gently as they followed Boone to his vehicle.

Dallas had to give the sheriff of Peaceful Valley, Maryland, credit. He had double the number of state troopers, DC officers and Montgomery County police in his office as he probably had on his entire payroll. Rather than being intimidated or territorial, he'd conducted the meeting and the interviews with the kind of humble confidence that must have made working with him easy. Thirtysomething years old with the kind of good-old-boy demeanor Dallas had seen in a lot of small-town cops, Sheriff William Mitchell had a keen mind, a sharp eye and a straightforward way of dealing with people. He sorted out who was who, offered everyone coffee, asked a few questions and then allowed the state police to take Michael into custody.

Within a half hour of arriving at the sheriff's office, everyone was leaving.

That was fine with Dallas. His knee throbbed with the kind of intensity that made him feel physically ill. Thanks to Michael, the knee had shifted, straining the healing meniscus. At least, that was what he hoped had happened. He didn't want or need another surgery. He was ready to get back to work and his busy life.

He wasn't sure how he felt about getting back to having a quiet house, though. After a week of people moving in and out, he was getting used to noise and action and conversation. He was getting used to being awoken by the sound of Zane trying to be quiet while he got a bowl of cereal, Carly's whispered warning to keep it down, the gentle swish of water through the pipes in the walls.

He was getting used to laughter—the kind of boyish giggles that hadn't been part of his life when he was young, the soft, warm chuckle when Carly was amused.

He was getting used to a lot of things. He was enjoying a lot of things, and he wasn't sure how he'd feel when the house went silent and the places that had been filled were empty again.

He took Carly's arm as they stepped outside, helping her across the icy parking lot. She didn't try to pull away, and he didn't want to release his hold. Not even when Boone unlocked his SUV and opened the back door.

"Better climb in," Boone urged, pulling a packet of small doughnuts from his coat pocket. "It's cold out, and your hair is still wet from earlier. Don't want it to freeze up on you."

Carly slid in without saying a word, and Boone closed the door again.

"What's going on with you two?" he asked as if it was a normal question. Blunt. Unapologetic. Typical Boone, but that didn't mean Dallas had to answer.

"We're going to the hospital to check on her friend," he responded, and Boone grinned.

"What?" Dallas demanded, heading around the front of the Jeep.

"You're avoiding my question."

"I'm not avoiding. I'm just not answering."

"Why not? Are you embarrassed that you're finally falling for someone?" He popped a doughnut in his mouth, not making any move to get in the driver's seat.

"More like annoyed that you think you know whether or not that's happening."

"I'm not claiming to know anything. I'm asking questions because I'm curious. You avoiding the questions makes me even more curious. It's a vicious cycle that only you can break."

"Then I guess the cycle will continue," he replied, climbing into the back seat.

Carly had her head against the window, her eyes closed. The gray morning light highlighted her cheekbones and the smoothness of her skin, the red-gold threads in her dark hair. She'd been mostly silent in the sheriff's office, her face a shade paler than normal, her body completely shrouded in the blanket. Now it had fallen away, pooling in her lap and onto the seat.

He tugged it over her again, reaching for the end of her seat belt and pulling it across her lap.

She grabbed his wrist without opening her eyes.

"I can do it," she said.

"Yeah," he responded, snapping the belt into place as Boone pulled out of the parking lot. "I know."

"And yet, you did it for me anyway," she said, finally opening her eyes. They were deeply shadowed, the months of worry and sleeplessness etching fine lines in their corners. She looked delicate, vulnerable, beautiful, but it was her strength that he saw most clearly—the fiery light in her eyes, the sardonic curve of her smile, the hint of sarcasm in her voice.

"Does that bother you?" he asked.

She hesitated. "Unfortunately, no."

"What's unfortunate about it?"

"That's a good question, Dallas. Get back to me in a few days, when all this is over and I don't have a hundred thoughts about a hundred things running through my head, and maybe I'll be able to answer it."

"Sounds like a plan," he said, going with his gut. Just like he always did.

"What sounds like a plan?"

"Getting together when all this is over and figuring out how we both feel."

She was silent for much longer this time, but he

didn't speak, he didn't try to rush her and he sure didn't give her reasons why getting together was a good idea.

He wasn't sure if it was a good idea.

He just knew it was what he wanted. He thought it might be what she wanted. Time together to figure things out, to try to understand why their lives before they'd met suddenly didn't seem like enough.

"Okay," she finally responded, her voice so quiet he barely heard.

He lifted her hand, brushing tiny bits of glass from her palm, then did the same for the other one. In silence, because there wasn't anything that needed to be said. They didn't need to discuss pros and cons, possible hitches to the plan. They just needed to take things moment by moment, trusting that they'd been brought together for a reason beyond the present circumstances.

God had perfect timing.

His parents had been feeding him that line for as long as they'd been in his life. After the car accident, he'd decided that God's timing stank. He'd looked at the photos of his wife, flashing on the overhead screen at the memorial service, and he'd thought about how horrible it was that God had put them on the wrong road at just the wrong time for three-fifths of the people he loved to die.

But there'd been other moments in his life. Moments when he'd moved a fraction of an inch just before bullets whizzed through the spot he'd been standing in. Moments when he'd hesitated at a green light and watched as a semitruck barreled through a red. Moments when he'd been right where he needed to be at exactly the right time to help someone who desperately needed it.

God had perfect timing. Even when the outcome of that timing hurt.

That last part had become his personal addition to his parents' mantra. Because either God was good, or He wasn't. Either He was giving the best to His children, or He was a liar. After months of wrestling with those two thoughts, Dallas had concluded that He was good, He was truth and He knew best.

But that didn't take away the sting of pain, the heat of anger, the bitterness of loss.

It didn't take away the resentment he sometimes still felt toward God, but it had helped him gain perspective. It had allowed him to move beyond the pain and to focus on making something positive out of the negative. Losing Lila and the twins had made him more determined to make a difference in the world. He was doing that every time he went on a mission. He was doing it each time he brought one of the missing home.

But there was more to life than that.

There were quiet times that begged to be shared. The first snowfall of the season, the tiny bird that had built a nest under the porch eaves, the yellow tomcat that sat on the porch railing and sang for his supper. In the past few months, he'd longed to put his arm around someone and watch the days go by, the weeks pass, the seasons change.

He hadn't thought about it much before. He sure hadn't prayed about it. He hadn't thought he really wanted it, but then Carly had started running past his house every morning, and one day he'd been pulled into her life.

He didn't want to step out of it, and he didn't see any reason why he should have to.

His phone buzzed, and he dragged it out of his pocket, saw Chance's number and answered. "This is Dallas. What's up?"

"We have a problem." His tone was clipped and hard, and Dallas tensed.

In all the time they'd known each other, he'd never known Chance to lose his cool. "What kind of problem?"

"I got a call from Sergeant Wright. With Raintree booked and heading to jail, she thought it would be safe to pull the guard that's been standing outside Jazz's room."

"I don't think I like where this is heading," he muttered, meeting Carly's eyes.

She mouthed, "Zane?"

He shook his head.

"I didn't feel comfortable with that, so I asked Stella to head over to the hospital and wait there until you arrived. She's there now. Apparently, Jazz is not."

His blood went cold at the news. "What is the hospital saying?"

"The fiancé made a stink, accused them of not having the neurosurgeon in quickly enough after she regained consciousness. He said he was taking her to Johns Hopkins, was able to sign the paperwork for her self-discharge because he has power of attorney."

"You've got to be kidding!" he said, knowing that Chance wasn't.

"I wish I was. Of course, we're all hoping that he really is on the way to Hopkins with her."

"But?"

"I had Trinity run his name and Michael Raintree's together. Just to see if we got any hits. She found a Facebook page for a private school in New York that both men attended. They graduated the same year. She's beating herself up for not seeing it before, but the post was hidden in the archives. Just a couple sentences from each about a scheduled reunion."

"It's not her fault," he said, but he wasn't focused on the conversation. His mind was racing through dozens of possibilities. "How long ago did they leave?"

"The paperwork was signed twenty minutes ago. He wheeled her out to his car himself, didn't even let her get dressed. Her nurse nearly had a coronary, but there wasn't anything anyone could do. The security guard at the door saw him help her into a black sedan."

"Do we have a make on the car? A plate number?"

"For what?" Carly had leaned across the bucket seat, her head so close to the phone, he could feel icy tendrils of her hair brushing his knuckles.

"I put a call in to Sergeant Wright. She'll be able to pull them more quickly than we will. I'm staying at the house with Zane. I don't trust that this guy isn't going to show up with guns blazing. Jackson will stay with me. You want to drop Carly off and then go on the hunt?"

"Yeah. Can you have Trinity send me the file of information on Brett Williams? I want to read over it. See if anything stands out to me now that I know he and Raintree are affiliated."

"No problem. You'll have it in five."

Chance disconnected.

"What happened?" Carly demanded, her voice sharp, edged with fear.

"Brett checked Jazz out of the hospital."

He saw the moment the truth registered, the way her eyes narrowed and her fists clenched. She might be terrified, but she was also angry, the pulse in the hollow of her throat beating frantically. "That makes more sense."

"Than?"

"Michael coming up with all this on his own," she said simply, pulling out her phone. "I wonder if he grabbed her bag before he kidnapped her."

"I know there's a reason you're worried about it. Want to share?"

"When Zane's kindergarten class went on its first field trip, I was freaking out. Jazz had a meeting in New York, and I couldn't chaperone. He was all I had, and I was terrified he'd wander away or be taken. Jazz bought a phone he could carry in the pocket of his cargo shorts and installed an app that would allow us to track him. We're both on it. I tossed her phone in the bag when I packed her things for the hospital." Her voice broke, but her expression didn't change. She typed something into her phone and smiled grimly. "And there she is."

She turned the screen, and he could see the small photos of Zane, Carly and Jazz on a map. She touched the photo of Jazz, and the screen zoomed in on her location. She was moving away from the hospital, heading northwest.

"Does Brett know she's on this?" he asked, typing her coordinates into a text and sending it to Chance.

"Probably not. He's a little…possessive, and Jazz has a habit of only telling him things that impact him. Otherwise, he likes to make decisions for her, and that drives her nuts."

"Sounds like a winner."

"Like I said before, I've always thought she could do better. I just didn't know she was with a guy who was capable of something like this. If I had..." She shook her head, frowned. "I think they're going to my place."

He'd been thinking the same, working through the coordinates on the map, the direction they were traveling and where that might lead them. "We'll drop you off at my place and then head over."

"That's time we can't afford to waste," she said calmly. "I'm going with you. I'll do what you say, stay in the car, hide behind trees, dig a tunnel into the earth and cover myself with snow, but I'm not going to slow down the rescue efforts by letting you bring me to your place."

He couldn't argue with her logic. And he couldn't come up with a good enough reason to countermand it.

But he wanted to, because he didn't want her anywhere near Brett.

"Sounds like a plan to me." Boone spoke into the silence. "Sergeant Wright should be close behind us. I'll ask her to keep her sirens off. I don't want this guy to have any warning that we're on the way."

"Right," Dallas said, punching in the sergeant's phone number and waiting for her to pick up, calculating in his head how much risk was involved in bringing Carly to the house, realizing that any amount of risk seemed like too much.

He wanted her safe, healthy, happy.

He wanted her out of danger and far away from anything that could hurt her.

Boone had accused him of being embarrassed because he was falling for someone. The truth was a little harder for Dallas to swallow and a whole lot more terrifying.

He wasn't falling. He'd fallen. Quickly, suddenly,

unexpectedly, he'd done the one thing he'd told himself he'd never do again. And the woman he'd fallen for was heading straight into danger.

He swallowed down panic, tamped down the desire to argue his case, force his will, make Carly do what she didn't want to.

But she was right. Forty minutes was a long time when someone's life was on the line.

The call went to voice mail, and he left a message, then settled back into his seat and mentally calculated the best route into and out of Carly's brownstone.

TWELVE

Things like this weren't supposed to happen in broad daylight.

In every movie Carly had ever seen, every news report she'd ever watched, the bad guys did their deeds in the darkest hours of the night. The heroes ran to the rescue when the sun was down and they had less chance of being seen.

Reality was a lot different.

Reality was parking a half mile from the house, watery sunlight filtering through the Jeep's windows while Dallas and Boone finalized their plan.

Or tried to.

"No," Dallas barked for the fifteen thousandth time.

At least, it seemed like that when time was ticking and Jazz was alone with a...

Killer?

Stalker?

Lunatic?

All of the above?

"You want to get in the back door without him noticing, right? The best way to do that is to have Carly go to the front door. She can call now. Tell Brett that she went to the hospital, heard he'd checked Jazz out. She's on the way home and wants him to meet her there, so she can see how Jazz is doing. He'll be waiting for her, watching out the front while you move in through the back. I'll be near the corner of the house, out of sight, waiting to take action if necessary."

"No," he repeated, but Carly was already dialing.

To Dallas's credit, he didn't try to take the phone. Instead, he just shot daggers from his eyes as the phone rang.

Brett picked up immediately. Of course.

"Where are you?" he demanded. "I've been waiting for hours."

"I ran into some trouble. You know my boss, Michael?"

"I don't have time for this, Carly," he growled. "Where are you?"

"No need to snap. Michael has been causing me some trouble. He may be responsible for what happened to Jazz."

"Where. Are. You?" he asked for the third time, his voice stone cold.

"I was at the hospital. The nurse told me you'd insisted Jazz be discharged because you didn't think they were providing the necessary care. Are you at Hopkins? I thought I'd stop by the house and get a few more things for Jazz and then head there. Dallas lent me his car, because my van is at his place and he's being questioned by the police."

"About what?"

"Like I said, Michael's been causing me some problems. Dallas has information about it. He's sharing that with the police. I figured while they worked things out,

I'd visit Jazz. Can you think of anything she might need from the house?" Her mouth was dry with fear, her words thick with it.

"Actually, I stopped by your place to grab a few more things. Great minds, right?" he said, his tone completely changed. He sounded warm and friendly and kind. Everything that he obviously wasn't.

Poor Jazz. She'd be devastated when she learned the truth.

If she didn't already know it.

Her fingers tightened on the phone, but she kept her voice light. "Exactly! Should I go straight to Hopkins, then?"

"No. Come here. Jazz would probably prefer you pack her bag. Are you close? I don't want to keep her away from the hospital for too long."

Lying piece of garbage was on the tip of her tongue. She managed to not say it.

"Maybe three minutes from the house. How is she? Can I speak with her?"

"She's resting. I think she'd rather stay here and forget the hospital."

"I can't say I blame her. Give her my love," she said, praying that Jazz was alive. That he hadn't already done something horrible to her.

"I will." He disconnected, and she was left holding the phone to her ear, listening to the empty connection and her own pounding heart.

"Good job," Dallas said quietly, all the frustration gone from his eyes. All she could see there now was compassion, understanding, worry.

"A B-list actress could have done better," she responded, and he smiled.

"I'm glad to see terror doesn't chase away your sarcasm. It's one of the things I like about you."

That surprised a laugh out of her. A harsh, rough, ugly laugh, but still a laugh.

"He's expecting me in about three minutes. That gives you just enough time to get to the back door. Be careful, okay?"

"I planned on saying the same thing to you. There should be some kind of police presence here soon. Chance sent me a text saying they're coming without sirens and lights. If Brett sees or hears them while you're at the door..."

He didn't finish. She knew he was thinking that things could go really bad really fast.

"I'd rather him not," he finally said.

"Then we should probably do this now. Before they arrive."

She tried to sound confident and unafraid, but she didn't think she fooled him.

He touched her cheek, just a gentle, light brush of his palm that skimmed the angle of her jaw. His hand settled on the side of her neck, his thumb resting in the hollow of her throat. She knew he could feel her pulse racing, feel the rapidness of her breathing.

"You're going to do great," he said calmly, and then he leaned in, brushed her lips with his, the caress as gentle and pure as the first spring rain.

She wanted to lean into him, linger for a moment longer, but Jazz was alone with a man whose agenda Carly couldn't even begin to understand, and Dallas was already moving away, climbing out of the Jeep and closing the door. She watched as he walked to the brownstone at the top of her street, rounded the corner of it and headed into the side yard. Seconds later, he'd disappeared from view.

"Ready?" Boone asked, and she met his eyes, saw a tough determination there that she hadn't noticed before. He'd seemed like the nice guy of the group. The good old boy. The one who wouldn't hurt a fly.

He didn't seem like that now.

Now he seemed focused, sharp and capable of just about anything.

"Yes," she lied.

"Okay. You'll drive to the house, park on the street across from it. You're not going to see me, but I'll be around. If anything happens, I guarantee you I'll protect you," he said, getting out of the Jeep, opening her door, waiting while she climbed into the driver's seat.

He didn't say another word as he closed it. Just gave her a quick nod.

Then, like Dallas, he walked away, taking the same path out of sight. She had to trust that both men would be in place before she arrived at the house, that everything they'd discussed would go off without a hitch.

She put the Jeep into Drive, her hands shaking so hard she wasn't sure she could navigate the snow-covered road.

"Please, God," she whispered out loud, a dozen petitions filling her head.

She couldn't put voice to them. They were a soundless, wordless prayer, swirling up from the depth of her soul, filling the empty air and rising to the ears of the One who held every moment in the palm of His hand.

This wasn't his idea of a good plan, but given the circumstances, it was the best one they had. Dallas waited until his cell phone buzzed, signaling that Carly was heading to the front door. Then he climbed over the fence and moved toward the back door.

There was no doubt Brett would be at the front of the house, watching for Carly. He'd probably be at the door when she arrived, pushing it open, greeting her with that polished, perfect smile of his. Dallas had pegged the guy as a snotty yuppie who had money and liked to let everyone know it. In the eight days Jazz had been hospitalized, Brett had had flowers delivered five times. The last time Dallas had been in the ICU, the room had smelled like a funeral parlor—dead flowers, musty water and Brett's overpowering cologne.

He hadn't liked the guy, but not liking someone didn't mean they were a criminal. There'd been nothing concerning in Brett's background, nothing that had made them stop and take more notice. On paper, he was a well-respected copyright lawyer who lived in a penthouse in New York City. He had an apartment in DC, a black Mercedes and a boat he kept docked at a marina on the Eastern Shore of Maryland.

Obviously, he had plenty of cash.

Or wanted people to think he did.

Money and greed were powerful motivators.

He reached the back door without a problem, pulled out the glass cutter Boone had taken from his glove compartment. He'd have preferred to use a punch. It was quicker and easier, but also louder. One quick hit and the glass would shatter, warning Brett of his presence. Slicing out enough of the glass to reach the doorknob was a slower way to go, but it was also quieter.

A soft hoot drifted from the front of the house—a signal that more people were arriving. The local police or more HEART members, probably. It didn't matter. The plan had been set in motion. He was going to follow through. Doing anything else could get someone killed. Carly should be at the front door by now, talking to Brett, making excuses for not entering the house. Stalling, because that was what she'd been told to do.

He duct-taped the glass near the lock mechanism and made the first cut, working quickly. He'd done this hundreds of times before, knew he could be in the house in seconds.

Somewhere to the left, a door opened. Footsteps padded on the snowy grass.

He spun in the direction of the sound, his gun in hand, the glass forgotten.

Jazz was there, swaying on her feet, sixteen shades of white. Gaunt and ghostlike and moving toward him in bare feet and a hospital gown. Her lips were blue and her eyes hazy, but she grabbed his arm, motioning for him to be quiet.

"I saw you from the living room. Would have gotten to you sooner, but that jerk fiancé of mine put something in my juice. Like I wasn't already loopy enough. Just like always, he's underestimated me," she said, her voice like a worn-out violin, the strings frayed, the sound scratchy and uncomfortable.

"I'm Dallas Morgan. Carly's—"

"Brother-in-law. I wasn't as out of it as everyone thought while I was at the hospital. Just couldn't get my mouth and body to cooperate. Not that I care who you are. I figure if you're at the back door while she's at the front, you're together. The side door is open. He won't be able to see you as easily if you go in through there. Carly's outside on the front stoop, but..." Her voice trailed off, and he wasn't sure if she'd lost her train of thought, or if she didn't have the heart to voice her fears.

They moved around the side of the house, the door into the kitchen wide-open. Boone stood at the corner of the brownstone, his back to them. He didn't acknowledge their presence, but there was no doubt he knew they were there. His focus was on the front of the house and on following through with his part of the plan.

"Stay here," Dallas whispered as they neared the side stoop, but Jazz had already slumped down in a heap of hospital cotton, shivering.

He shrugged out of his coat and dropped it over her, wanting to do more, but the clock inside his head was ticking, counting off the minutes. Carly had no idea her friend had opened the door for him, no idea she could turn and walk away and leave Brett in the empty house.

The plan had been for him to open the door, walk in and take Brett down.

She was expecting to see Dallas, to step away once she did. Quickly, without giving away his presence.

"What did you do?" a man shouted.

A woman screamed, the sound cut off as a gunshot broke the morning silence.

Dallas's heart jumped, adrenaline speeding through his blood as he stepped through the kitchen and ran for the front door.

THIRTEEN

Everything happened at once.

A police car pulling up the street. Brett seeing it. His eyes going wide and then narrowing. His shout. Boone running around the corner of the house. Metal flashing. The world exploding. Boone falling back, getting up again.

Carly trying to run, Brett's hand fisting in her hair, pulling her back and tossing her into the house with so much force she slammed into the wall. A framed photo fell, the glass shattering, and then the front door was swinging open and Boone was running inside.

Cold metal pressed against Carly's temple, and she was yanked to her feet. Unsteady and confused, Brett's arm tight around her waist, she looked straight into Boone's eyes. He didn't look nearly as terrified as she felt.

"Get out!" Brett growled. "This isn't your business."

"It's my business anytime a punk like you tries to harm someone," Boone responded, blood oozing from a wound in his upper arm.

"I said," Brett hissed, "get out."

"Sorry. I'm not one of your hired lackeys. I do what

I want. You might as well let her go," he said reasonably. "The police are here. You're going to jail. Better to get booked for assault than murder."

"I'm not going anywhere, and I'm not getting booked for anything," Brett responded. "Back up, or I'll put a bullet in her head."

"No, you won't," Boone said, blood seeping through his coat and trickling down his arm. Voices drifted in from outside, mixing with the tinny sound of a police dispatcher answering a call for backup.

Brett had to know he'd lost, that whatever he'd hoped to accomplish wasn't going to happen, but he kept the gun pressed painfully to Carly's temple, his arm clamped around her waist.

"I don't make idle threats," he spat, the gun digging deeper into Carly's skin. "Stay there and let me do what I have to."

"What would that be? Bully an unarmed woman? Drag an injured one from the hospital because you're too much of a chicken to face the consequences of what you've done? Is that what you want? To go free so you can do the same thing to someone else?" Boone was talking, dragging out the conversation, probably trying to keep Brett's focus toward the front of the house.

Had Dallas made his way in?

She hadn't heard glass breaking or doors opening. She hadn't heard footsteps, either, but she knew how silent he could be.

"What I want is for you to shut up," Brett snapped, jerking Carly backward a couple of steps.

Was Dallas behind them?

That had been the plan. That he would come in through the back and take Brett by surprise.

"So it *is* money," Boone said, looking about as bored as anyone in the middle of a hostage crisis could possibly look. "What'd you do? Get in too deep with the New York underground? Do you owe the wrong people money? From what I hear, they don't much like it when they don't get paid. They're liable to kill a man for not producing the cash when it's time."

Something he'd said hit its mark. Brett stiffened, and then he shouted, "I said, shut up!"

He swung the gun toward Boone, and that was all the opportunity Carly needed.

She swooped down, grabbing a shard of glass, the razor-like piece slicing through her palm as she came up swinging. Pain speared up her arm as she punched hard, the glass digging into Brett's biceps.

He cursed, firing blindly, the bullet flying wild as someone barreled into him from behind.

Dallas.

They tumbled onto the ground, rolling into the coffee table.

And then the world went still and silent as Dallas knelt over Brett, pressing the barrel of a gun to his jaw.

"I suggest," he growled, "that you not even breathe heavily."

"You won't shoot me. I'm not even armed anymore," Brett sneered, his gaze darting toward the gun that had fallen from his hand. It lay near the stairs, bits of glass glittering nearby.

"If you want to test that theory, go for your gun," Dallas retorted.

"Police!" an officer shouted, racing into the room, gun drawn. "Put your weapon down!"

Dallas did as he was told, setting the handgun down and pushing it away.

"Keep your hands where I can see them and step to your right. Over near the recliner." The commands were clipped and sharp, the officer's gun swinging from Dallas to Brett and back again.

Everything should have been easy from there. Cuff the bad guy, frisk him, read his Miranda rights, all of it as polished and predictable as a new penny.

Except that Brett moved, his hand snaking out, his body rolling over.

He had the gun and was up as the officer shouted the command for him to stop, and then Dallas was moving, too, diving toward Carly, wrapping his arms around her as the world exploded.

One gunshot. Two, and she was on the ground, Dallas's weight pressing her into the floor. Her head was against his chest, and she could hear his slow, rhythmic heartbeat, sense the moment when he started to move. Feel her own heart slowing as she realized he hadn't been shot. She hadn't been shot, and Boone...

She tried to lift her head, but Dallas felt like solid steel. Two hundred pounds that felt more like four, and she could barely breathe.

"I'd like to live," she managed to gasp. "Oxygen is a requirement for that."

"Boone?" he said. "We're good. You can get up anytime you want."

"Be easier to do if I weren't bleeding like a stuck pig," Boone responded, apparently on top of the small mountain of humans they'd become.

He rolled to the side, managed to make it to his feet.

She couldn't see anything but his black boots and the cuffs of his pants. There were drops of blood on both.

"He needs an ambulance," she said as Dallas put a hand under her elbow and helped her to her feet.

"I need food. Some kind of stew would be nice. With some homemade bread on the side," Boone retorted, probing the hole in his coat. "I don't think this is as bad as the bleeding makes it seem. The bullet went right through the fatty part of my arm."

"You don't have fat on your arm," she said, and he grinned.

"Yeah. Like I said…stew would be nice."

"I'll make you a pot after you're out of the hospital."

"You're not going to be doing much of anything with your hand like that." Dallas eyed the deep gash in Carly's right palm. Thick rivulets of blood flowed out of it, dripping down her knuckles and onto the floor.

She'd had worse cuts, and she shrugged off his concern, tried to step past him to look for Jazz.

"It's probably best if you wait outside," he said, and she realized he'd positioned himself between her and Brett. Boone had moved into position just a few inches behind him. They were purposely blocking her view. She craned her neck to see around them, caught a glimpse of feet. Legs. Brett's body lying still on the floor.

Dead?

She thought so, but she didn't have the guts to ask.

"I need to find Jazz," she said instead.

"She's outside. There should be an ambulance on the way."

"Is she…okay?"

"She said he put something in her juice. She was

shaky but lucid when I was talking to her." He edged her toward the door, and she went, because whatever Brett had done, whatever he'd been involved in, whatever had caused him to turn on people he supposedly cared about, she didn't want him to be dead.

She gulped cold, clean air as she walked outside, tried to tell herself that everything was okay. That the police had the person who'd been blackmailing her, that all the bad times were over, but then she saw Jazz, sitting on a blanket in front of the house. Dallas's coat lay beside her, and a police officer and an EMT crouched beside her.

She wasn't looking at either of them.

Her gaze was on the horizon, her body turned slightly away from the house. She looked lonely and lost and sad, and Carly's heart broke into a million pieces for her.

"She's going to be okay," Dallas said, his hand on her elbow as he helped her down the slippery front stairs.

"You can't know that."

"Yeah. I can. Because she's your friend, and you're going to make sure she is. Besides, she's tough and resilient. Like you."

"I don't feel tough. I feel tired," she said.

"I guess you won't be up for a run on my favorite trail, then. Don't worry, though. I can think of plenty of things we can do together," he said with the sweet, gentle smile she was beginning to love.

"Like what? Hide in snowy fields and avoid bad guys?"

He chuckled. "I was thinking more along the lines of hot chocolate and warm fires. You, me and Zane watching old Christmas movies together."

"That sounds nice," she said.

They reached Jazz as two ambulances sped up the road, sirens blaring, lights flashing.

Jazz didn't seem to notice. She was still staring into the distance, her face paper white, her eyes hollow.

"Hon?" Carly said, crouching in front of her, touching her cheek and then smoothing the tangled hair from her forehead. "I'm so sorry this happened."

She nodded but didn't speak, and that was almost worse than anything else, because Jazz always had words and songs and smiles, and now she was just an empty shell of herself, sitting in the middle of snow-covered grass.

"Are you in pain?" Carly asked, reaching for Dallas's coat.

He was already lifting it, setting it around Jazz's shoulders over a blanket the EMT had already placed there.

"I'm not the one bleeding," she responded, her voice raspy and worn. "Did he do that to you?" she asked.

"No. I did it to myself."

"You're going to need stitches."

"All I really need is to know that you're okay," she responded.

Jazz finally met her eyes. "I will be. Eventually. Where's Zane?"

"At Dallas's place. With some of his coworkers."

"Sounds interesting," she said, her gaze cutting to Dallas.

"Not really," she replied, her throat burning with tears she refused to let fall.

"Liar." Jazz's voice was gentle, her expression soft.

"Maybe some of it is interesting," Carly admitted, grabbing her hand and holding it, as if she could will some life and warmth and joy into her. "I'll tell you stories on the way to the hospital."

"I'd rather just stay home," Jazz said, her gaze shifting to the brownstone and the police milling around it. "He's dead. Isn't he?"

"I…"

"Saying it can't make it worse. Or better." She pulled her knees up to her chest, resting her head against them as the ambulance crew approached. "So just tell me. Is he dead?"

Carly glanced at Dallas, and he offered a quick nod.

"Yes. I'm so sorry, sweetie." She dropped her left arm around Jazz's shoulders, hugging her because she couldn't offer anything else.

They sat like that while the EMTs worked, while Carly's hand was wrapped and Jazz was asked a dozen questions. While Boone was loaded into an ambulance and more police cars arrived. They sat for what might have been minutes or hours, and when the gurney was rolled across the grass, Carly still didn't want to let go.

"You can ride in the ambulance with her," Dallas murmured in her ear, his hands on her shoulders, his breath ruffling her hair.

"Are you coming?" she asked, allowing herself to be led away from the crew that was strapping Jazz in.

"Do you want me to?" he asked.

"Does a wildflower want sunshine?" she replied without thinking, and when she heard him chuckle, she realized what she'd said.

"What I mean—"

"Tell you what, Carly," he said, turning her so they were face-to-face. "How about you explain what you meant while we're watching those movies and drinking that hot chocolate?"

She almost kept backtracking and offering words that would have meant absolutely nothing. But Jazz was being lifted into the ambulance, and an EMT was asking if Carly planned to ride along, and…

And Dallas was staring into her eyes, waiting for her to respond.

"Okay," she finally said. She saw him smiling as she turned away, knowing that for once she'd made the right choice.

He walked her to the ambulance, waited while she was helped on board.

"I'll see you soon," he promised as the door closed.

And after hundreds of promises that had been made to her during her life, hundreds that had been broken, she suddenly knew what it felt like to have faith in another person, to believe without a shadow of a doubt that what he said was what he would do.

FOURTEEN

Neither Carly nor Jazz had been willing to spend another night in the brownstone.

Instead, they'd found a weekly rental and started looking for another home.

They'd moved into it a week before Christmas, relocating from the city to a farmhouse thirty miles away. It was a long commute, but Carly had spoken to the new director of operations at the Smithsonian, and he'd been eager to allow her a flexible schedule. They'd agreed to four ten-hour shifts. It was tough, but doable. She took the Metro in and back most days. Her contract would be up in six months, and she figured she could do anything for that long.

Of course, she was already being offered a salaried position. With nice pay and good benefits.

She was thinking about taking it.

Her cynical side thought the Smithsonian was offering her the position because it was afraid of bad publicity. She couldn't help thinking that the director thought keeping her close would keep her quiet. If he'd asked, she would have told him she had no intention of talking.

With Brett dead and Michael in prison, she had no reason to do anything but move forward.

Although she wouldn't be able to do that completely until Michael's trial ended.

He'd pleaded not guilty to charges of attempted murder, extortion and attempted kidnapping. He'd been telling anyone who cared to listen that he'd had nothing to do with any of those things. Like Carly, he'd been blackmailed by Brett. They were old friends, and when Michael and his wife decided to adopt their second child, they'd contacted Brett to find out if he knew anyone who could help shorten the process. Brett had put them in touch with an international adoption agency that worked in South America. Less than nine months later, they had a son. A month after the baby was placed with them, the agency closed and the owners disappeared. There were whispers of child trafficking, federal charges and stolen babies, but Michael and his wife weren't contacted by the police, so they went on with their lives and tried to put the experience behind them.

And then Brett had called. He needed cash to pay back a debt he owed. Gambling money that he'd never be able to repay. He'd told Michael that if he didn't help him out, the police might come knocking on his door, asking about the baby's adoption.

Terrified, Michael had given him what he'd asked for, but it hadn't been enough. Brett had been well connected. He'd heard about the Smithsonian's newest collection of antique jewelry and the estimate of its value, and he'd come up with a plan to get his hands on it.

Or that was what he'd told Michael, anyway. No one would get hurt. The forged jewelry would be nearly identical to the original pieces. It could take years for anyone to discover the truth. No harm, no foul. He'd outlined the plan, including hiring Carly and having her forge the gems. She'd be the perfect scapegoat if anyone noticed the forgeries. If anyone ended up in jail, it would be her. That was what Brett had said, and he'd seemed happy for that to happen.

Michael had gone along with the plan because he'd had to, but the longer things went on, the more he'd begun to suspect that Brett was more interested in getting Carly out of his life than he was in selling jewelry for money.

It was possible that was the truth. Brett had taken ten thousand dollars in cash from one of his accounts. The man who'd been apprehended at the hospital had deposited five thousand in cash the morning before the attack. A second man had been arrested at a Virginia hospital where he'd gone to have an infected gunshot wound treated. His blood type matched that found at Dallas's house, and he'd confessed to being paid to follow Carly, take photos of her son and send her anonymous messages. The police suspected he'd set the fire at the brownstone and that he'd been attempting to kidnap Zane. A metal bat had been found in the trunk of his car, and they believed it was the weapon he'd used to attack Jazz.

The fact that Brett had taken out a one-million-dollar life insurance policy on himself and one on Jazz had added to the police speculation. He'd also talked her into allowing him to have power of attorney if anything were to happen to her. Jazz had said he'd done it all under the guise of preparation for their marriage. In reality, he'd owed a lot of money to men who'd been eager to collect, men who weren't known

for their patience. The police speculated he wanted
Carly out of the way because she was the only family Jazz had. Without her around, there'd be no one to
question an accident or a suicide.

She frowned, lifting a string of garland from a box
and weaving it around the mahogany banister on the
front staircase. Dawn had barely touched the sky with
gold, and she was up decorating, because her in-laws
were coming over to spend the day.

She wanted to be happy about it, but she wasn't feeling very festive. Neither was Jazz, but Sarah had asked
if they could spend Christmas Eve as a family—baking
cookies, drinking hot chocolate, cooking Christmas
dinner, going to Christmas Eve service, spending time
getting to know one another. Dallas's mother had been
so sweet about it, so kind that Carly hadn't the heart
to say no. Even if she had, she would have agreed. She
and Jazz weren't feeling festive, but Zane was.

He'd been talking nonstop about Christmas for
weeks. When he wasn't talking about it, he was in his
room with the door shut, making Christmas gifts for
all the people he loved.

Apparently, that list was much longer than it had
been in previous years.

It had taken two packing boxes to carry the gifts
to their new home. Carly hadn't been allowed to help.
Zane had asked Dallas to transport them.

Dallas…

He was taking up a lot of her thoughts, filling a
bunch of empty places in her heart that she'd barely
even realized were there. The fact that she didn't mind,
that she wasn't putting up roadblocks and building walls
and trying to keep him at a distance should have scared

her, but this was Dallas she was putting her hopes in, and the only thing she felt when she was around him was happiness.

She eyed the garland, decided it looked good enough and walked into the living room to grab a few red velvet bows from the coffee table. The room was cold, winter air seeming to seep in through the windowsills. Unlike the brownstone, the farmhouse needed some work. It was functional and sturdy rather than fancy and polished. She liked that. Still, she hadn't planned to buy it. She'd been leaning toward something modern. A new townhome a little closer to the city, maybe, but Jazz had seen the old house while she was doing a real estate search, and she'd told Carly they needed to see it.

So, of course, they had. Anything to get Jazz out of the house. Anything to make her smile. It had been a hard few weeks for her. She still had migraines from her head injury and pain from her shattered collarbone. She still had nightmares. She still sat in front of the window and stared out at nothing.

She'd told Carly repeatedly that she was healing, that she felt okay, that she was going to be just fine. There was no mistaking her sadness, though. Nothing she could ever say would convince Carly that she wasn't heartbroken and mourning.

Brett had been a horrible person, hiding a secret life that Jazz had known nothing about.

But she'd loved him. A person couldn't just turn that off.

Carly knew that firsthand.

She'd hoped that the house would give Jazz something to focus on. They'd talked about decorating it, and Jazz had even managed to pull the Christmas boxes out of the pile of storage items they'd stuck in the walk-up basement.

She hadn't opened any of the boxes, though.

As far as Carly knew, she hadn't done any drawing or designing since the accident. She hadn't been to church, hadn't talked to friends, hadn't done anything but pretend she was okay.

Carly's cell phone buzzed, and she glanced at the screen, smiling when she saw that Dallas was calling. He'd be returning to work after Christmas, and that seemed to be his excuse for spending as much time as he possibly could with her and Zane. As if he needed an excuse.

"You're up early," she said, and he chuckled.

"Says the woman who's awake at five every day. What are you up to?"

"Hanging garland, trying to get ready for your parents' visit."

"Have I thanked you recently for allowing my parents to be part of today?"

"You did. Last night, yesterday afternoon. Yesterday morning. And I keep telling you there's no need to thank me. I'm happy to include them."

"And dreading it, too?"

"You know me well, Dallas," she responded, laughing a little as she tied a red velvet bow to the garland. "I'm an introvert. I like my space, but I also like your parents, and I want them to enjoy their grandson."

"They love Zane, but that's not why Mom wanted all of us to spend the day with you."

"No?"

"My twins were due on Christmas Eve. It's a difficult day."

Her heart dropped, and she sat on the steps, the garland and bows forgotten, everything out of her head but Dallas and his loss. "I'm so sorry, Dallas. I thought they were probably due around this time, but I didn't want to ask. It seemed too personal."

"It's not something I talk about often, but I wanted you to know."

"Is there anything I can do? Besides be here for you?"

"Spend tomorrow with me. Mom always has a big Christmas bash to try to distract me. I'd love it if you, Zane and Jazz would come."

"Zane and I will be there. I'll try to talk Jazz into it. She's been a little…down."

"I know. I've been thinking about that, trying to come up with something that might help. Last night, an idea came to me. If you open the door, I'll explain it."

"Open the… You're here?" She nearly flew across the foyer, unlocked the front door and stepped into his arms. He smelled like leather and snow and winter fires, and he felt like home.

She burrowed closer, wrapping her arms around his waist, holding him tight as if that could somehow take his sorrow away.

"I'm just so sorry, Dallas," she whispered, her head against his chest.

He stroked her hair but didn't speak. His muscles were tense, his movements tight.

There were no words for his kind of grief. She knew that, and she let the silence settle.

Wind blew in through the still-open door, but she didn't reach to close it.

She waited, holding him as tension eased from his muscles, as his hands slid to her waist. When he kissed her, it was sweet and tender, gentle in a way no kiss had ever been before. And when he finally broke away, she wanted to pull him close again.

"Thank you," he said, his voice gruff, his eyes dark.

"For the kiss?"

"For being here. Last night was rough. I've been driving around since midnight, and I finally decided I wanted to come to the only place that has felt like home since…" He shook his head. "I missed you," he finished, and she let that be enough for both of them.

"I missed you, too. Which is funny, since I saw you—" she glanced at her watch "—less than ten hours ago."

"Ten hours is a long time," he said, finally smiling. "Is Jazz still sleeping? I want to show you what I got for her."

"Yes," she said.

"No," Jazz corrected, walking down the steps, her jeans and T-shirt baggy around her gaunt frame. "It's Christmas Eve. We need to decorate this place up. Right, sport?" she called, her voice so overly cheerful it was almost painful to hear.

"That's right!" Zane called, racing down after her, his blue pajama bottoms an inch too short, his hair spiked up around his head. "We haven't even hung the stockings yet, Uncle Dallas! You want to help?"

He didn't wait for an answer, just ran to the nearest box and started digging through it, pulling out one Christmas item after another.

"At least one of us is having fun," Jazz said with a tired grimace. "You're here early, Dallas. Want some coffee?"

"Maybe in a minute. I brought something for you, and I don't want to leave it in my car for much longer."

"For me?" Jazz said, her gaze darting to Carly. "What is it?"

"I have no idea. He was about to tell me when you came down."

"Wait here. I'll bring it in," Dallas said, walking back out into the blue-gray morning.

"Why would he get me something?" Jazz asked. "Because he pities me? That's the last thing I want."

"No one pities you."

"No, you just feel sorry for me. It's pretty much the same thing." She sighed, smoothing her hair. "It better not be a coupon for counseling. Or a tub of ice cream. If one more person tells me I need to eat, I'll scream."

"Ice cream?" Zane shouted. "Are we having that for breakfast?"

"No. Your uncle got a gift for Jazz. He's about to bring it in. She thought it might be ice cream."

"Or counseling," she muttered.

"I bet it's even better!" Zane said. "I bet it's a pink pistol."

"What would I even do with that?"

"Shoot bad guys?"

"He wouldn't get her a gun," Carly cut in, trying to reroute the conversation.

"Oh! I know. I think it's a clown, because clowns make people happy."

"I'm happy," Jazz said.

Zane put his arms around his aunt's waist and hugged her. "You will be. Once you have a clown."

"Whatever it is," Carly said, "it's taking him a long time to get."

"That's because," Dallas said, stepping back inside and closing the door, "it wasn't all that keen on leaving the car."

"It?" Carly asked, frowning as something beneath his coat wiggled.

"What is it?" Zane whispered, taking a step closer.

"He," Dallas corrected, reaching under his coat and pulling out a bundle of black-and-white fur. "I found him at the local shelter a few day ago. It looked like he needed a little extra love."

"A puppy!" Zane gasped.

"A puppy?" Carly repeated, even though she could see very clearly that it was.

"You brought him for Jazz, so he can stay with us, right?" Zane said, reaching out to touch the puppy's nose. It licked his hand, and he giggled.

"Yes. If she wants him." He glanced at Jazz. She hadn't said a word. Maybe she was thinking it was a pity gift. Maybe she wasn't interested in taking on the responsibility of a puppy.

Carly shouldn't have been interested, either. Their lives were busy, and a puppy was one more thing to worry about, but it was the cutest puppy she'd ever seen, its eyes dark brown, its fur thick and soft looking.

"If she doesn't want it," Dallas continued, "I'm sure I can find it another home."

"Your place?" Carly guessed, and he shook his head.

"I'm not home enough. It wouldn't be fair. One of my coworkers might be interested. A couple of them have kids, and this little guy would be great to grow up with." He set the puppy down, and it shook itself out, then scampered across the wood floor, skidding as it tried to stop.

"Does he have a name?" Zane asked, laughing as the puppy grabbed a red bow and sprinted across the room with it.

"Moose," Jazz said suddenly, and the puppy's floppy ears perked up.

"What?" Carly asked, surprised to see a half smile curving the edges of Jazz's lips.

"His name is Moose."

"Moose like the animal? Or Mousse like the dessert?" she asked as though it really mattered, and Jazz's smile broadened.

"Like the animal, because that will make people smile, and I'm realizing that smiles aren't always that easy to come by." She sat on the floor, crossing her legs and patting the floor. "Moose. Come!" she called, and the puppy ran right to her, climbing into her lap and jumping up to lick her face.

She kissed his nose and patted his head, then called Zane over to pet him. While he did, her smile stayed in place, her eyes shining with it.

"Wow," Carly said quietly, whispering in Dallas's ear. "That's the first time she's smiled in almost a month."

"She hasn't had a lot to smile about," Dallas responded, hooking an arm around her waist and pulling her close. "Are you angry?"

"About the puppy? Why would I be?"

"It probably wasn't the best idea to let Zane see him before I consulted with you."

"I'm pretty sure you knew I wouldn't be able to say no. Even if Jazz didn't want him."

"You do have a soft heart," he murmured.

"And a big enough house to fit an army of puppies," she responded.

"Are we getting more puppies?" Zane asked excitedly.

"Let's just enjoy this one for a while," Jazz said, her expression soft and unguarded, her cheeks pink with pleasure.

It gave Carly hope to see her like that. It made her think that maybe Jazz really would be all right.

"You look happy," Dallas murmured.

"I am. Are you?" She searched his face, tried to find some hint of the memories she knew were haunting him somewhere.

"I'm always happy when I'm with you."

"I'm happy when I have coffee," Jazz interjected. "Maybe one of you can make a pot while Zane and I entertain our new friend."

"I'll do it," Carly offered, walking toward the doorway that separated the living room from the hall, Dallas right beside her. It felt good having him here. It felt like joy and peace and contentment. It felt like all the dreams she'd had as a kid coming true, all of her prayers being answered.

It felt like love, and she wasn't too afraid to admit it, because it was nothing like what she'd had with Josh and everything like it should be.

"Stop there for a second, Carly," Jazz called.

Surprised, Carly did as she asked, glancing over her shoulder and smiling when she saw Moose sitting in Jazz's lap, staring at her adoringly—floppy ears and huge paws, big brown eyes and scrawny body under puffs of wool-like fur.

"Do you want me to try to scrounge up some food for him while I'm in the kitchen?" she asked, assuming that was what Jazz wanted.

"I have a fifty-pound bag in my trunk," Dallas said. "And a few toys. And a stuffed dog that's supposed to make him not miss his littermates. Actually, I may have gone overboard and bought most of what they had in the pet store near my house."

Carly met his eyes and grinned, suddenly caught in his gaze, in his gorgeous eyes and amused expression.

"Perfect," Jazz said. "But I hadn't even thought of food for Moose. I just wanted to give Dallas an opportunity to take advantage of the situation he was about to find himself in."

"What situation?" Carly asked, and Jazz pointed to the area above her head.

Carly looked up—and saw a sprig of mistletoe hanging from a hook above the door. "Because true love's kiss," Jazz continued, "can be as elusive as a smile."

"True love's kiss, huh?" Dallas took Carly's hand and pulled her close. His palm was warm, his gaze somber. "I like the sound of that."

"Me, too," she responded, and he smiled.

"Should we give it a try?"

"The kiss?"

"True love. With a kiss thrown in for good measure."

"I can't think of anything I'd rather do," she responded, laughing as Moose ran past, a velvet bow tied around his neck, Zane racing after him.

She was still laughing when Dallas kissed her, the warmth of his lips promising all the things she'd ever wanted: a lifetime of friendship, of laughter, of puppies and of kisses under the mistletoe.

* * * * *

Don't miss these other
MISSION: RESCUE *stories*
from Shirlee McCoy:

PROTECTIVE INSTINCTS
HER CHRISTMAS GUARDIAN
EXIT STRATEGY
DEADLY CHRISTMAS SECRETS
MYSTERY CHILD
THE CHRISTMAS TARGET
MISTAKEN IDENTITY

Available now from Love Inspired Suspense!

Find more great reads at www.LoveInspired.com

Dear Reader,

In the silence of cold winter nights and the hush of snowy winter days, I often find myself thinking about Christ's birth, about the way it must have felt to be Mary or Joseph or the shepherds in their fields. None of those people were rich or beautiful or well liked by the world. They were poor and humble and even despised.

The Christmas story is told so often, depicted so frequently, that it is easy to become immune to it, to forget how miraculous the birth of Christ was, how life changing, how world changing. The message of His birth and life and resurrection is not one of divisiveness and hate, but one of love. This Christmas season, I hope you have a chance to slow down and look around, to see with fresh eyes the beauty of the world you live in. Take a walk through an icy forest, explore snow-covered paths or—if you live in warmer climates—stand on the beach and look at the vastness of the ocean and the sky. He is there with you, my friend, in all that great and wild beauty, and in the smallest, darkest place in your heart.

Blessings,

Shirlee McCoy

Get 2 Free Books,
Plus 2 Free Gifts—
just for trying the
Reader Service!

SPECIAL EXCERPT FROM

Love Inspired.
SUSPENSE

*When danger strikes at Christmastime,
K-9 FBI agents save the holidays and fall in love
in two exciting novellas!*

Read on for a sneak preview of
A KILLER CHRISTMAS by Lenora Worth,
one of the riveting stories in
CLASSIFIED K-9 UNIT CHRISTMAS,
available December 2017 from Love Inspired Suspense!

The full moon grinned down on her with a wintry smile. FBI Tactical K-9 Unit agent Nina Atkins held on to the leash and kept an eye on the big dog running with her. Sam loved being outside. The three-year-old K-9 rottweiler, a smart but gentle giant that specialized in cadaver detection, had no idea that most humans were terrified of him. Especially the criminal kind.

Tonight, however, they weren't looking for criminals. Nina was just out for a nice run and then home to a long, hot shower. Nina lived about twenty miles from downtown Billings, in a quaint town of Iris Rock. She loved going on these nightly runs through the quiet foothills.

"C'mon, Sam," Nina said now, her nose cold. "Just around the bend and then we'll cool down on the way home."

Sam woofed in response, comfortable in his own rich brown fur. But instead of moving on, the big dog came to an abrupt halt that almost threw Nina right over his broad body.

"Sam?"

The rottweiler glanced back at her with his work expression. What kind of scent had he picked up?

Then she heard something.

"I don't know anything. Please don't do this."

Female. Youngish voice. Scared and shaky.

Giving Sam a hand signal to stay quiet, Nina moved from the narrow gravel jogging path to the snow-covered woods, each footstep slow and calculated. Sam led the way, as quiet as a desert rat.

"I need the key. The senator said you'd give it to me."

Nina and Sam hid behind a copse of trees and dead brambles and watched the two figures a few yards away in an open spot.

A big, tall man was holding a gun on a young woman with long dark hair. The girl was sobbing and wringing her hands, palms up. Nina recognized that defensive move.

Was he going to shoot her?

Then Nina noticed something else.

A shallow open pit right behind the girl. Could that be a newly dug grave?

Don't miss
CLASSIFIED K-9 UNIT CHRISTMAS
by Lenora Worth and Terri Reed,
available wherever Love Inspired® Suspense books
and ebooks are sold.

www.LoveInspired.com

Love Inspired®

Inspirational Romance to Warm Your Heart and Soul

Join our social communities to connect with other readers who share your love!

Sign up for the Love Inspired newsletter at **www.LoveInspired.com** to be the first to find out about upcoming titles, special promotions and exclusive content.

CONNECT WITH US AT:

Harlequin.com/Community

 Facebook.com/LoveInspiredBooks

 Twitter.com/LoveInspiredBks

LISOCIAL2017